I0547711

# BREATHLESS 5

# *LOVING JACOB*

by Shani Greene-Dowdell

All Rights Reserved

Copyright © 2017 Shani Greene-Dowdell

All rights reserved, including the right of reproduction in whole or in part in any form. Without limiting the rights under copyright reserved above, no part of this publication may be reproduced, stored in or introduced into a retrieval system, or transmitted, in any form, or by any means (electronic, mechanical, photocopying, recording, or otherwise), without the prior written permission of both the copyright owner and the above-stated publisher. The scanning, uploading, and distribution of this book via the Internet or any other means without the publisher's permission is illegal and punishable by law. Purchase only authorized electronic editions and do not participate in or encourage electronic piracy of copyrighted materials.

This is a work of fiction. Names, characters, places, and incidents either are the product of the author's imagination or are used fictitiously, and any resemblance to actual persons, living or dead, business establishments, events, or locales is entirely coincidental

**<u>Read the Breathless Series in Order</u>**

Breathless: In Love With an Alpha Billionaire:

Breathless 2: In Love With an Alpha Billionaire:

Breathless 3: In Love With an Alpha Billionaire:

Breathless 4: Loving Montie

Breathless 5: Loving Jacob

Breathless 6: Drive Me Wilde

Breathless 7: In Love With an Alpha Billionaire

# Chapter One

## Destiny

### *Like You Used To...*

I looked at the old, run-down building Tasha called a lounge and shot a disgusted look in her direction. "I don't know why I let you talk me into coming out here. I should be in bed after the long day I had with Junior's game. And I have to get up and take care of my family tomorrow, you know?"

I had no clue what it would take to make the latter come true. With the raging feeling in my gut that Jacob had done the unthinkable with Justine, I wouldn't rest well until the truth was unveiled or the nagging thought got put to bed, once and for all.

"It may look a little worn on the outside, but trust me, Destiny. This is exactly what you need right now," she assured me. Part of me wanted like hell to believe her. "And you'll see it's not a bad place when we get inside," she added as she strutted ahead of me, wearing a pair of cute, six-inch heels and her head of ringlet curls bouncing in the wind and cascading down to her ample bottom. My cousin, Tasha Baker, had dolled up like she stepped off the pages of a fashion magazine just to take a walk through the pearly gates of hell. I would never understand why.

"Tasha, I don't want to be here!" I protested with a permanent scowl taking up residence on my face.

She stopped walking and spun around to face me with fire shooting from her eyes. "You're the one who said you needed to relax and clear your mind. That's what we're going to do, so stop putting down the one place where you might be able to relax tonight. The building looks one way, but the vibe is on another level. Just wait and you'll see." She turned and stalked across the street as quickly as she faced me.

"Well, I tell you I'm suspicious of Jacob and Justine, and you bring me *here* to get mugged? I can see how this is what I need," I stated sarcastically, smacking my teeth like I used to as a little girl while continuing to follow her. Our heels clacking against the gritty pavement only reiterated my discomfort with the dingy, broken-down venue.

There were probably fifty cars in the parking lot and a few parked alongside the road. The streets were dark, except for one dim lamppost. Jacob's security detail was nowhere in sight, so I successfully ditched them on the drive to Tasha's house earlier. I had intentionally zigzagged through traffic and made sudden turns to lose them. Thankfully, it worked. I needed a breather from Jacob's protective watch.

"I'm getting tired of your bitching, Destiny!" Tasha said, bringing my attention back to her. "You need to come down a notch. You may live in The Hills with Jacob now and have forgotten where you came from, but I haven't forgot your lil' snotty nose trotting around following me everywhere I went on Benson Ave. So please, miss me with that highfalutin mess. It won't work with me, because I know you," she said as she slowed down to walk by my side.

"Where I live has nothing to do with this bummy place. I'm just saying, why did we have to come here?" I hopped over a puddle of dirty water in the walkway...well, at least I hoped it was water. It could've been—hell, no. I just hoped it was water. "Really, Tasha?"

"Wait until I tell Moneefa that you act like you haven't seen a water puddle before. I remember when we used to pray for rain so we could play in the rain and the water puddles it left behind. Now you're too bougie to step over a puddle," Tasha said as we reached the door where a big, burly man started running a metal detector over her purse.

"I am *not* bougie!" I said as the man took his wand and started waving it over my bag. I snatched my purse from his reach, and he humped his shoulders. "This is just a sleazy place," I added.

"Hold up, lady. I have to pat you down, too," Mr. Burly said, and I was one hundred percent sure he was harassing me as retribution for my harsh words about the death trap of a building he guarded.

After nearly every orifice of my body was touched by a man I didn't care to ever see again, I walked into the smoky club with my stomach churning with revolt over the dank mixed cigarette smoke that filled the air. Women barely wore clothes, and dread-headed men were everywhere, including posted up against the walls.

"This is your idea of what I need right now?" I mumbled loud enough for Tasha to hear as I stomped behind her like a petulant child. "I'm starting to think you don't know me that well, Tasha."

Tasha stared at me with a dead look. She pursed her lips together as if she were willing herself not to respond. Just like she knew me well, I knew Tasha. She was ready to strike with venom.

"We're not going to be out here, Destiny," she said. "I'm taking your uptight ass to the poetry lounge in the back, but if you keep bitching and moaning about it, I'll take you back to my house, so you can get your car and go home. I'm tired of hearing about it."

"Whatever." I looked around at the collard green colored walls with more paint chipping away than remaining.

*Maybe I am acting a little bougie. Maybe I have forgotten where I came from.*

Those thoughts made me quietly pull about ten stairs behind my bestie cousin, who had never led me astray. I was met by an entirely different vibe once we entered the poetry lounge. A lady with a long, curly afro stood at the mic in front of a vibrant crowd in a rustic, culturally decorated small room. Everyone was laughing, talking, sipping drinks, and enjoying the vibe.

"Oh damn, help me welcome back one of Miami's finest adopted poets, Poetically Tash!" the emcee shouted in our direction, and the crowd roared with applause and whistles. Tasha halted to blow the emcee a kiss. "We need her to grace the mic tonight, so y'all gotta do a little better than that," she said and the crowd roared with cheers and clapped even louder.

*Well, I'll be damned.*

Tasha didn't tell me she was a spoken word artist. There's a lot of mystery about my favorite cousin. When I figured my own life out, I planned to take the time to spend more time with Tasha, peeling back her layers. Maybe even find out why she had no trace of a man.

After purchasing much-needed relaxation in a glass, we found a table in the center of the room and sat down. I ordered a margarita, and Tasha ordered a mojito.

"So, you come here a lot?" I asked as we got comfortable in our seats. My interest raised, wanting to know more about the type of woman my first female role model, close to my age, had grown into.

"Yeah, I do, actually."

The people in that room knew and loved her. She nodded in the direction of a man sitting across the room waving at her. A girl stopped by our table wearing a dashiki shirt, fitted jeans and African designer shoes and hugged Tasha's neck. They briefly caught up and the colorfully dressed woman left our table.

"I didn't know you were into the spoken word," I said.

"Yeah, and stop looking at me like that."

"Like what?"

"Like me spitting poetry is something insane. I like writing and getting shit off my chest. This is a good outlet for both," Tasha defended.

"I didn't say there was anything wrong with it. I know you're a journalist, but I'm astounded by the fact that you are into the arts like that," I said, taking another sip from my glass.

"Whoa, little cuzzo is *astounded....*"

"Yes, I am," I giggled, "...and I'm even more ecstatic that I'll see you perform tonight. In that case, I thank you for bringing me here, and I take back every other thing I said about this...place." I looked around at people vibing to sultry jazz music, and for the first time, I felt good about being at that club.

"Uh, not going to happen. I brought you here to listen to some of the other uplifting, righteous poets in Miami. I'm not gracing the mic, though," she said, shaking her head as if to shake the thought far away from her.

"I know you're not chickening out because I'm here. If you're scared, say you're scared," I challenged while chanting our old anthem.

"*You* calling me scared? That's funny when I'm the one who's been on that same stage in front of more knowledge-hungry, woke people than you have ever spoken to publicly.

10

How about *you* get up there and spit something?" She crooked her neck and tilted her head as she sneered at me.

She hadn't asked me a question. She issued a threat.

I scanned the room, clearly intimidated by the group, some sporting afros and wearing dashikis, others wearing braids and the latest fashion trends. It was a crowd of mixed backgrounds and mindsets, and I wasn't afraid of them from where I sat. It was a different ball game to get up on that big stage and have them all look to me for something thought-provoking. The thought sent shivers ricocheting through my chest. *What would I say? How would I sound?*

Instantly, I was afraid of my own voice.

My lips moved. A lie exited. "I'm not scared to speak in front of these people, girl. Are you serious?"

Tasha challenged my flippant response. "Prove it, and go sign up for open mic."

"So, the open mic is open?" I asked, almost babbling the words on top of each other. The last thing I wanted was to get up there and make an utter fool of myself. I would sound like a gibbering idiot if I did. "I mean, is it open to anyone?" I corrected myself.

Tasha hit the table with the palm of her hand as she laughed uncontrollably. "Ha! You're funny, and you're scared as shit. Of course, the mic is open. That's why they call it *open mic,*" she mimicked, making air quotes with the two final words.

Laughing with her to show I could take her joke, I took another sip from my drink. It was damn near empty now. I needed another one.

"What are you gonna do, Mrs. Bougie?" Tasha broke into my thoughts. "You gonna get up there and say what's on your mind, or will you back down after all of your big talk?"

I looked at the stage and took in a gulp of air. I had made the faux, bold assertion that I was braver than she thought, so I had to roll with it. "I'm not backing down, smart ass," I told Tasha. "I'll speak my mind on the 'open mic,' no problem."

*What in the hell was I saying?* Of course, I was backing down. As in, right now backing down...and leaving this place in my rearview, even if that meant calling a cab.

"Well, go sign up then," Tasha urged, pointing to the sign-up table near the door. I had obviously overlooked the lady standing at the table by the door when we arrived minutes earlier.

"I think I will sign up just to show you that you're not the only one with talent." I stood up and stalked little by little toward the lady standing by the door.

I didn't write poetry, much less perform spoken word, so I had no valid reason to chunk myself out into the void of the spoken word world. I suddenly felt like a kid again, back on the playground with Tasha and her friends, being pressured to do something I did not desire. I learned from those experiences that I could do anything if I pushed myself to do it. I always showed her I could do anything she could do.

By the time I finished my thoughts, my name was on the dotted line of the sign-up list, and I was about to debut as a spoken word artist.

*Now that you've signed up, run for the hills... literally.*

Ignoring the negative thoughts swirling around in my head, I walked back to the table, thinking about what I would say once my name was called. A lot of drama was happening in my life that I could address—Montie arguing with me about Junior's game and pressuring me to be a better co-parent, and Jacob keeping something secret that my gut told me had to do with Justine.

No matter how good it would feel to pour the woes out of my soul into the thirsty crowd, Jacob was well known in Miami as a real estate billionaire. I couldn't very well get up there and talk about our marriage without one person in the audience recognizing me. If no one recognized me, at least one video recording would get out and reveal my identity later. Therefore, I had to be discreet in my messaging.

"There's my shit-talking cousin," Tasha said once I returned to the table and my chair went screeching across the floor, so I could sit down. She tilted her drink in my direction and asked, "Did you really sign up?"

"Of course, I did, honey. I do what I say I'm going to do, which in this case should be lots of fun." I tilted my glass in her direction with the fakest confidence I could muster. Forget spoken word; I should've gone into acting.

"Listen, Destiny, I talked my junk, but you don't have to embarrass yourself by getting up there on stage. No one is forcing you to do anything you're not comfortable doing, so right now is the perfect time to back out. I'll get my girl to scratch your name," Tasha said as I settled in my seat across from her.

"Oh, don't worry about me. I got this. I can back up anything that I say. I'm good," I lied straight through my chattering teeth.

Jacob's picture flashed across my phone screen. I sent his call to voicemail. Seeing his face usually gave me a vote of confidence, but his cream with just the right amount of cinnamon tone in the message didn't envelop me and warm me to the core like a cup of hot coffee. His deep-set hazel eyes didn't allure me into another realm of reality. We were off, and until he opened up about Justine, we would remain this way. She mentioned too many details about our home the last time we had a run-in with her at Jacob's mother's house. Yeah, my so-called loving mother-in-law just couldn't bear to cut ties with her friend's insane daughter, but that's another story.

Jacob's eyes caught mine and fluttered away that night we saw Justine. He could barely hold my gaze. My powerful man, known for wearing a poker face, broke down on the inside. His body language spoke to me and awakened a million insecurities I had at the beginning of our relationship with Justine.

Later that night, he assured me Justine only knew intimate details about our home's interior because his mother told them to her. However, even his mother hadn't been in our bedroom and study.

*Damn you, Jacob!*

My heart screamed as I looked down at his picture again. A scowl spread across my face as I internalized the possible indiscretion I talked myself into believing.

*No way. There's no way he slept with her.*

I just couldn't believe it.

"Alright, go ahead and be a word gangsta then," Tasha was saying when my mind returned to the room, bringing my attention to my pledge to get in front of an unfamiliar crowd and speak. She tilted her drink toward me for a toast. "I like that about you, Destiny. You have always been willing to take one for the team," she added and chuckled.

I tipped my drink her way and downed the margarita. I went to the bar and got a glass of red wine. A few more songs vibrated from the speakers, and a few more spirits tranquilized me before the host returned to the stage to send my nerves raving again.

"We have our roster filled for tonight with powerhouse oldies and some wet behind-the-ear newbies coming your way. I want to shake things up and bring a newbie to the stage first tonight. Would you guys like that?" the host queried the crowd.

"Bring on the new blood," a man sitting close to the stage yelled.

A resounding "yeah" came back from the remainder of the audience.

"Alright! Let's get started. The first sister came through the door with Poetically Tash, so I'm sure she's bringing the heat. Let's snap it up for her as she comes up to the stage, y'all. Come on up and give us what you got, Lady Des."

Yeah, I gave myself a stage name, and my heart dropped into my panties when she called it. But a woman of her word does what she says she's going to do and does it to the best of her ability.

I rose from my seat and stole one last gulp from my wine glass. I floated to the stage, arriving without remembering the trip there. I took the mic from the holder and immediately greeted the anxious crowd.

"How is everyone tonight?" I must have spoken too softly. Only a few people answered. "I said, how are y'all doing?" I said louder.

"Goods, fines, and lovelies" returned from the once again lively audience.

"Well, I'm a little nervous. This is my first time performing at an open mic, and to top that off, I've never spoken the words I'm about to say to a soul. They are not rehearsed, and I've never written them anywhere. What I have to say comes straight from my heart to your ears," I said and rubbed my palms together. "Okay, so here goes," I exhaled a heavy breath.

"Speak your mind, girl!" I heard a woman yell.

"Take your time, sister," a male's voice accompanied hers.

I closed my eyes and just allowed my subconscious to flow with impunity...

*"Baby, I'm starting to feel like*
*You don't want me like you used to*
*I remember when I would walk*
*Into a room and your whole world would change*
*It was as if you already had me on your brain*
*Your best friend couldn't stand me*
*The look in your eyes made it plain for her to see*
*The spell I had over you could not be broken...*
*The days of your heart roaming from this lady to the next was revoked*
*All conversation would cease as I walked toward you*
*I was the air oxygenating your every part*
*Oh, the intricacies of your tough and tender heart*
*You'd feast your eyes upon me*
*As if you were anxiously awaiting my touch*
*Yearning to feel my body next to yours*
*The desire within you burned so deep*
*Where did that part of you go*
*Did it die, or is it asleep*

*Maybe I'm starting to lose my glow*
*Am I too refined...*
*Is my age starting to show*
*When I walk into a room now*
*You see me, but don't make eye contact*
*Instead of reaching for me, you turn your back*
*Barely acknowledging my presence*
*From the looks of things, it would appear*
*You'd rather I not come near*
*How did we get to this place*
*How do we get back and erase...."*

Something magnetic jolted inside of me. I opened my eyes and scanned the room in search of Tasha, then stilled at the profile of the man I knew soul to soul. My poetry-spitting lips halted as my breath caught. *Jacob.*

The audience clapped and snapped, thinking I paused for effect, demanding more. Jacob's dark, searing eyes insisted the same. A tear fell down my cheek as I silently challenged him with the same two questions that ended my piece.

Then, I found Tasha's face in the crowd. Her big eyes and sincere smile told me she coached me to the stage to bare my raw feelings so Jacob could hear. Or was it a simple case of him having his security follow me everywhere I went? Maybe I didn't lose them like I thought I did.

Either way, snaps ricocheted throughout the room, bringing my attention back to the stage where I stood locked in panic. I looked into Jacob's curious eyes again and gave him and the crowd what they wanted, more.

*"Your attention, I'm constantly wanting*
*Our passion's fire can't be allowed to die*
*The thought that we could ever be over, the devil is a lie*
*The fire in our souls is destined to catch*
*You bring the gasoline baby and I'll bring a match*
*Let us live in truth...*
*Let's be lovers and do what lovers do*
*This day*
*...all day*
*...and baby all night*
*I want you*
*To want me*
*Like you used to*
*But it has to be true."*

The room erupted in a firestorm of snaps and claps, and one woman yelled, "He better come correct or keep it moving!"

"If he don't do you right, I will," a handsome young man wearing a blue blazer and jeans said after the racket died down.

"Hold on, buddy. It's just a poem. I'm doing right by her now and forever," Jacob responded to the man as he walked to the edge of the stage where I exited. "We need to talk," he said close to my ear, clasped my hand in his and started toward the door.

"Jacob, I came here because I needed time away from home."

"What's that poem about?" he asked, continuing the beeline down the stairs and toward the front of the club. "You know what, don't answer that. Once we leave here, you will have all the time you want, either to yourself or talking to me." He stepped in front of me and opened the front door. "This is no place for you to be hanging out. When Tallen told me you were on this side of town, I immediately had Henry drive me over. You know this isn't safe."

*So, Tasha didn't tell him where I was. It was Tallen from his security team.*

"My God, Jacob! You see for yourself that it's a relaxed crowd. There is nothing wrong with this place," I said, suddenly on the defensive side of the poetry spot's beat-up building I'd spoken so ill of upon my arrival.

"Well, you've had your time away. I hope you enjoyed yourself. It's time to go, so I can show you I do *want you* more now than ever. I didn't realize you felt neglected or that I had gotten so distant from you."

"You didn't have to have me followed to figure that out, Jacob."

"You're going to have security with you until I feel you're safe without it. That's non-negotiable. If there's one thing this whole ordeal with Justine's ex being found murdered taught me, it is that I would be crushed if anything happened to you, Montana, or Junior. You three mean the world to me.

I'll do whatever is necessary to keep you safe, even protecting you from yourself." Jacob tugged my arm and pulled me down the sidewalk toward his car.

"I don't want to be followed everywhere I go."

"I feel better having security protect you when I'm unavailable."

"Speaking of available. I thought you had an important meeting you were attending."

"Destiny, I'm available to come to you at the drop of a dime. All I have to do is hear of some funny business like you coming to a club on the west side, and I will end a meeting with a filthy stinking rich Japanese supplier at the snap of a finger. Mr. Fukui can wait. I'll finish our meeting whenever we're good. After hearing what's on your mind tonight, I'm not so sure about us being good, and I don't like being unsure about anything."

I started to walk away from him, but he grabbed me by the waist and drew me back to him. Standing behind me with his arms holding me in place, he yanked me around and forced me to face him. "What was the meaning of your poem in there?"

"I have a lot on my mind."

"The meaning?"

"I didn't even know that would come out like that."

"The meaning, Destiny. It's obvious something's going on in your beautiful mind that's bothering you," he touched the side of my face. "You've been pulling away from me, and I don't understand why you would do that when you know I'll never let you go."

"It's not me pulling away," I told him, spitting fire into his orbs from mine. "It's you."

"I would never pull away from you. As much as I crave to be with you every moment of the day, that's the least of your worries."

"Yeah? Well, what did that look in your eyes mean that night when Justine mentioned the colors in our bedroom and study? You looked like the life had been siphoned out of you. Since then, you've been overbearing and had security hovering over me when you're not home. They follow me everywhere I go like there's something you're hiding and don't want me to find, more so than for my protection."

"There is something I need to tell you," Jacob said, his voice freefalling, dropping octaves as he spoke. "We can't talk about it in this parking lot, though. Let's go."

Judging by the aloof, remorseful look he bestowed upon me, what he had to say would be explosive. He promised he'd always be truthful, and I promised him the same once we entered our marriage. I had the unnerving feeling his truth would be our undoing.

## Chapter Two

## Jacob

### *Let's Get Away*

I nodded at Henry; he knew where to go and what plans to put in place. Once we turned onto the highway, Destiny sat up in her seat.

"Where are you taking me? I thought you said we were going home. If you must return to your meeting, that's fine, but I don't want to go with you. I'm too tired to be around more people," she asserted.

"This is important. There's something I would like to show you."

"Can't it wait until the morning? I'm tired from my long day, and we already have a lot to talk about," she said and yawned.

My heart fluttered a few beats as I watched the woman I loved lay back on the seat, spent, and look at me with need in her eyes. Destiny needed me to protect her. I internally grappled with how I would be able to do that while coming clean to her about Justine.

"No, like I said, what I must do is very important. It can't wait. I'll take you where you can relax shortly," I said and eyed Henry, so he would step on it.

My lady was growing impatient and I couldn't have that. We were headed to my private jet, where Junior and Montana were waiting for us. I had instructed Lynetta to prepare them for a few days away from home, and she would accompany us to care for them.

Destiny snapped up in her seat and surveyed her surroundings before spinning her neck in my direction. "It looks like we're going to the airport. Why are we going to the airport that houses your jet, Jacob?"

"I want to take you somewhere. Lynetta is bringing the kids to meet us, and I'm taking us away for the next twenty-four hours. I called Lynetta to set this up as soon as you began your poem. It looks like we're leaving town ahead of schedule of what I planned for this weekend, but this has to be done."

"Jacob, why are you talking in circles? I came clean to you about Montie. It hurt me to tell you that truth. I did it because I wanted to be open and honest with you. If you have something to tell me about Justine and you, skipping town will not help. There's nowhere you can take me that will soften the blow. No specific place will remove the nagging feeling that something dreadful is on the horizon for us," she said.

I turned her face and placed a soft, lingering kiss on her sweet lips. Her essence, combined with mine, linked us in an eternity of tenderness I was unwilling to let go. She rescued me from the routine of cross-country business meetings, meeting family expectations, and self-applied pressure to create the best portfolio in my family's history. Destiny showed me raw emotions, feelings, and beauty that money can't buy in day-to-day life. I had to have her for the rest of my life.

I pulled her into my lap to fill her with all I had to physically give as a symbol of everything I wanted to be for her and more. When she didn't resist my touch, my fingers went rogue, running from her tangled locks to the crease of her plump backside. I struggled to maintain control of my actions. We did have to talk, but I could show her how much I cared for her better than I could tell her. A deep sigh escaped my lips as I pulled away from her and looked toward the jet.

"Right now, I'm just asking you to trust me, Destiny. I will explain everything when we get where we're going." Henry opened the back door and Destiny's hot body slid from my lap into the seat, leaving me feeling cold and alone. I got out and held out my hand to her.

She sat frozen and defiant.

"Get on the plane with me, my love."

I hoped what I planned would remind us how deeply our love flowed for one another.

Destiny had a faraway look in her eyes as she slowly reached her hand to me. "I trust you," she said once she stood in front of me.

I read far between the three words, and her admission cut through my heart like an obsidian blade.

"All I have ever wanted to do is trust you with all my heart," she continued, slicing my deceit once again.

I touched the side of her face and stared into her peering eyes—a lovely shade of brown. Her beauty wouldn't be able to hide the hurt that would surface once she knew the truth. The woman I fell hand over foot for should never understand such pain on my watch. Still, I had to tell her everything after showing her how we got to this place to start with.

# Chapter Three

## Jacob

### *Atlanta*

I had Henry take Lynetta and our sleeping kids to the hotel while I loaded Destiny into the car I had readied for our arrival. I fired up the chocolate brown Jaguar XJ and breezed through the city toward the downtown area.

"Where are you taking me?" Destiny asked as we turned onto the street where we met. "Jacob, why are we at Tazi's restaurant?" she asked.

"Chocolate mousse cake."

"Really Jacob? This place is closed and we could have eaten cake in Miami."

"But it wouldn't have been Tazi's mousse cake." This place was sentimental for us. I expected we could rekindle what we meant to each other on that neutral ground.

"We can be anywhere and love each other, Jacob. Coming here in the middle of the night won't fix us if we're broken. I wouldn't know because you haven't told me what you have to say yet. We have to be honest with each other at all times." She eyed me suspiciously.

Another piercing-like strike went through my heart. *Fuck it.*

I opened my mouth to tell her the whole story about Justine sneaking into our home and seducing me while making me think she was Destiny. What did I have to lose? I could tell the truth and convince Destiny she owed me a second chance just like I gave her one after she slept with Montie, or I could continue lying by omission and have the suspicion hang over us until Justine blurted it out, leaving me looking like a two-faced cheater.

"Look, I'm not proud of what I've done," I sighed. "I have to tell you about that day when the lights went out in the city. I was alone in my study and she—"

"Are you two love birds going to come in or not?" Tazi Jefferson, the owner of the bakery's voice, infiltrated my slightly cracked windows. She stood at the door of her establishment, peering out at us.

I rolled my window down the rest of the way and said, "Yes, Mrs. Tazi. We're on our way in. Give us a moment."

"Alright, I have everything just as you requested and a little extra. Park in my private parking deck so you don't get towed. I'll buzz you in there." She watched us a little longer before returning to the store and behind the counter.

Destiny sat with her arms folded across her chest. After she waved at Tazi, the semi-smile she had retreated into the confines of her stoic facial features.

I loathed that she was holding her natural beauty from me. But I didn't loathe her retracting smile as much as I abhorred ever laying a hand on Justine, much less sharing intimacy reserved for my wife. I had yet to understand why I couldn't discern between the two women. I had to agree with Destiny on one thing, something was off about the situation.

"Are you going to explain why you brought me across state lines for cake when my only request was to have a heart-to-heart conversation with you?" she spat.

"My love, I figured the best place to make that happen would be here...the place where unsuspecting people sat for hours, bared their naked souls as strangers and by the end of the night, were inseparable."

"Jacob, I love you so much." A tear slipped from her right eye. I reached across the seat, arms stretched wide and eager to embrace her. She waved me away. "Don't...It shouldn't take all of this for you to say nothing happened between you and her. Just fucking say it!"

"I love you, Destiny. I love you and you only."

"Then tell me—"

"Dammit!" I grabbed her face and seized her lips. I kissed her with every bit of passion in me. She struggled to get away from me and murmured her protest against my lips.

I wasn't having any of it. I had to express my love for her in a universal language. Something she would understand better than what I was about to tell her. I allowed my tongue to let her know how deep my love flowed for her. She resisted until she had no win against the fiery passion shooting through me into her spirit.

When she let out a deep, throaty moan, I withdrew from her and drove into Tazi's personal parking garage, where only her BMW was parked. The double doors came down behind us.

I rushed to Destiny's door, pulled her to her feet, and into another kiss. Deepening the kiss, I felt my body come alive for my wife. My heart seemed ready to explode in my chest when I growled like a fierce lion, opened the backseat, and lowered her onto the seat, never taking my lips off hers.

She writhed against me, attempting to sit up. "No, Jacob. We can't do this here."

"We can. Watch me." My cock thrust against the fabric of my pants as I tore her shirt open and buttons flew across the car.

"Jacob, we can't—" she managed to rasp out through hazy passion from her flawless brown skin. She closed her eyes tight, clenched her legs together, and attempted to sit up again.

I yanked her pants down her legs and quickly discarded every article of her clothing. I slid my hand down to her neatly shaven pussy and grabbed it whole into my hand.

"I want you now."

"Jacob...baby...no, you can't do this."

"Is that right? Tell me I can have you now," I demanded as my tongue glided across her pretty flower and began flickering her sweetly scented bulb. "I'm not a begging man, but I'll do it for you," I said, licking her bulb one last time before I slithered my tongue up her stomach to her breasts. "Tell me."

"No."

"So, you're going to make me beg?" I asked before my tongue entered her mouth and tangoed with hers, mixing her essence in the hot pot of passion brewing between us.

"Can anyone see us?" she asked, her constitution withering.

"No, we're in here alone. Just the two of us."

Her legs spread eagle, and her hands flung around my waist, pulling me into her as she growled out a mix of anger and lust.

My head nestled in her nape. I unbuttoned my pants, pulled them down below my waist, cupped her voluptuous hips in my hands, and filled her sweet cunt to the brim. I sucked her neck hard, leaving a new mark of my love, alongside the many others she had in various stages of healing.

I kissed circles around the bruises and basked in the splendor of her sweetness. She didn't deny me what I hoped would always be mine, and I was a fortunate man for that. We would get through the storm ahead. It was a must.

"I will always love you, Destiny," I said, kissing her lips thoroughly. "Forever, I will love you more than anything on this earth."

"I love you, too, Jacob."

"Forever?"

"Forever," she answered, and if it was even possible, she coated my cock with more of her sugary juices and rode my waves from below in perfect harmony.

I snuggled my face against hers, inhaling her exhale as I slammed my dick into her tight walls.

"Oh, Jacob!" she cried out as I pounded at a pace that caused her to get wetter and hotter than ever.

"My pussy is so good," I told her. "Give me that sweet pussy. Give it all to me, my love. All of it."

"Harder," she muttered against my ear, and I thought I would lose all the good sense the Good Lord gave me.

"Take it all, my love. It's all for you," I answered her request with a vigorous pounding into her tender hole.

I roared like a raging maniac as waves of decadent bliss took me on to the promised land. The full length of my dick entering and exiting her suctioning cunt excited me to no end.

My balls tightened. Her melodic moans and whispers summoned the cum out into her fertile womb.

As I unloaded my seeds into her welcoming cove, her powerful release squirted onto the seat. Her body shook as hot cum gushed into her canal. We were trying to get pregnant, and I hoped that would be the moment I unleashed a winner inside the woman I loved. I wanted to give her a baby, so we would be bonded by our love evermore.

## Chapter Four

## Destiny

My gut told me to demand to be taken home. However, I lived in the moment and followed Jacob inside Tazi's Cafe in downtown Atlanta wearing only a tank top with his jacket covering it. We had more important things to do than eat dessert. Yet, there I was, lagging a step behind my man as we walked into the cafe. He reached his hand back to bring me close to his side.

"Come on, baby," he looked at me like he did the first day we met, and I melted instantly.

Why was I melting instantly when I needed answers he refused to give?

Jacob approached the counter in a measured stride. The sneaky grin on the white-headed woman waiting for us let me know she either saw us having sex in her parking garage or had an instinct that we were doing it.

"Hello, Mrs. Jefferson, so great to see you again," Jacob spoke.

"Hey, Son. Glad to see you love birds again," she smiled from ear to ear and winked at me.

*She saw us.*

"Thanks to your good cakes, I met my sweetheart, who I will love the rest of my life, right in front of your shop." Jacob's hazel eyes were on fire when he looked at me, singeing every spot on my skin he'd kissed in the car.

To stop the shockwave of heat surging through my body, I said, "Hello, Mrs. Jefferson. Nice to see you again, too."

"Oh, you two can stop it with that Mrs. Jefferson mess. Destiny, sweetheart, come over here and give Mama Tazi a hug," she said, smiling and opening her arms widely. I walked into her embrace and she hugged me, tugging me side to side. "You look beautiful," she said once she released me.

"Thank you," I blushed and leaned closer to Jacob's side.

"Now, Jacob, I have everything ready for you," Mrs. Jefferson noted, walking back behind the counter to grab a tray of her devil food. "...and you know I stayed late just for you, honey. Wouldn't even do it for President Obama, but your grandmother was such a good friend of mine, so that makes you family."

"Uh, I appreciate you setting up everything I asked for on such short notice," Jacob motioned with his hand to the table we sat at the first time we visited Tazi's. A unity candle like the one at our wedding sat in the middle. "...but would you pack it in carryout bags for us? Destiny is extremely tired and I don't want to keep her out any later." Jacob squeezed my hand before giving me a quick look.

"Oh, that'll be no problem. I bet she *is* mighty tired, Jacob," Mrs. Jefferson hinted, glancing at me with bobbing eyebrows and a telling smile.

*Hell yeah, she saw us.*

I shook my head. Jacob and his huge appetite would get us in trouble one day.

"We're just going to take our food back to our room and make it a late-night treat," Jacob said.

I discovered his plans for me as Mrs. Jefferson learned of them. I thought we would spend the night in his Atlanta condo, but I guessed he knew better than to take me back to the place Justine attacked me when so many questions about her hung in the balance.

Jacob looked at me and saw my eyes were locked on his soft, hazel green gaze. He didn't acknowledge my confusion. He just continued talking with Mrs. Jefferson as he looked at me.

She bagged our food and handed over two piping hot coffee cups, which Jacob suggested we needed because it would be a long night.

We thanked Mrs. Jefferson and stayed until she locked up. The three of us left together.

Jacob and I arrived at the Marriott Marquis. He picked up the keys to the penthouse suite at the desk. We went up to the top floor, and he unlocked the suite we made love in the very first time. Beautiful memories from the first night he touched me inside and out washed over me. Ironically, it was the first day we met.

If anyone had told me I would have bumped into the heir of Turner Enterprises and be in the billionaire's bed by nightfall, I would have cursed them out for suggesting that I was that kind of woman. I didn't fall in bed with men and say, 'oops here's a free coochie night for you, and you, and you....' No. That wasn't my way.

But Jacob...

He went from my instant lover to the heart of my heart, a friend and most sacred, my husband. We all think our hearts are under control until we're buried knee-deep in the confines of another's warm soul and never want to escape.

I scanned the lavish gold-trimmed penthouse, high-back chairs, and other regal furnishings. Was all of this meant to be a part of my life? Should I have turned him down when he asked me to come up to his room the first day I met him? Was I made for his world of power and privilege? Could a man like Jacob be true to me, and only me, for a lifetime like he'd so carelessly spoke about at Tazi's? I had so many questions.

Jacob had learned to be persuasive from his father, who learned to be dismissive and aggressive from his father. His family groomed him since he was old enough to walk to be a boss. He exuded powerful influence in the boardroom and in the bedroom. He had the ability to cause me to forget what I was supposed to be doing, finding out answers about him and Justine.

I glared into Jacob's piercing stare. He was used to getting what he wanted. I had the distinct feeling he knew telling me whatever he had to say would change that. Questions floated through my mind that dared to leave my lips. Feeling a cool chill float through the room, I crossed my arms over my chest and shivered.

Jacob sat on the edge of the bed beside me.

"I know you're wondering why I brought you here," he began.

"I have a pretty good idea why we're here, Jacob. We've already made out in Tazi's parking lot, so it's not that you wanted to take me in our first bed of love. You obviously want to be on playing grounds where you can use our history as leverage when you tell me what it is you have to say."

I prepared myself mentally for the worst. Perhaps, he still loved Justine, the bat shit crazy bitch who tried to kill me and probably murdered her ex-fiancé who left her at the altar.

"That's partially right, Destiny." Jacob stood up and went to the closet. "Here's something for you to wear to bed." He held a slinky white robe out to me that would barely reach down far enough to cover my ass, and it was low cut in the breast area.

"Deja vu." I held the tiny piece of fabric on one finger. "At least the first time you brought me here, you gave me your robe with some fabric. This little thing will barely cover me, and I'm sure it will be uncomfortable." I twirled the stringy material in my hand while shaking my head.

"Actually, it's too much fabric, but you can wear my robe if you insist. I want you to be comfortable, but not as bad as I want to see you in that gown."

I laughed. "Thanks. If there was less fabric on this gown, you'd only be able to call it a tampon?"

"Heavens no, I would never bring you anything to wear that would clog up that sweet hole?" Jacob smacked my bottom as I stood up to get his robe out of the closet.

I threw the gown back at him and it hit him in the face. He caught it as it fell and put it up to his nose and inside his mouth. He bit down on the paltry fabric, saying, "This would taste and smell so much better with your scent on it." His eyes raked over my body, displaying a desire to pounce on me with ravishing hunger like he did in his car.

I stood beside the bed with his robe draped over my arm. "You're stalling. Will we talk about what you brought me here for, or not?"

"We *are* talking. Have I ever told you that you make me the happiest man alive?"

"Yes, you just did in the car," I said.

He rubbed the spot beside him on the bed where he'd plopped down. "Come sit beside me, babe."

"No, I'm fine right here. What is it that you have to say?"

"Don't make me sit you down, Destiny. You know I will."

"You can't tell me what to do. I'd just rather go to sleep since you're not going to address what I want you to, and that's Justine's trifling ass still trying to interfere in our marriage and you acting like you've seen a ghost every time we see her. Do you think I don't notice how your demeanor changes, and it's not how I would expect it? Something is not adding up."

I walked around to my side of the bed and pulled the covers back. I slipped my dress off and slid on the robe.

Jacob did the same, undressing on his side of the bed.

"You'd better not touch me when you get in this bed," I warned him as I slid underneath the covers. "The only thing you can do in this bed tonight is talk."

My words drifted away as he slid underneath the covers and ran his warm hands over my neck, admiring it as if it were a perfect sculpture. He then ran his fingers through my hair and pulled my face to his.

Looking into my eyes, he crushed his lips against mine before I could flip in the opposite direction. Rogue moans escaped my throat, making him think it was okay to continue his assault on my lips.

He had no right. I wanted to talk, not make love. Which, of course, was why my arms nestled around his neck as our tongues danced to our own symphony. Powerful tension between my curvaceous thighs mounted to epic proportions for the second time that night. Being helpless to the overwhelming sensitivity emerging in my love cove pissed me off and drove me crazy at the same time.

The way Jacob owned my mouth spoke to his insatiable craving to unnerve me. This was his realm where he prospered. His greedy eyes spoke to me, urging me not to resist us. This was his way of communicating to me that he would always be true.

My hands left his neck and roamed freely over his body, leaving no place I could reach untouched. When I stroked his extended erection, he roared in anticipation of more than a touch. Surely, he didn't have anything to tell me that would break us. If he did, he wouldn't keep seducing me. At least, I hoped I was right.

*My husband has been faithful to me. I just know he has.* I kept telling myself that, over and over, as I fell back on the bed and allowed him to have me for the second time that night.

Once the robe was on the floor, he tossed the covers back, sprang to his feet, and removed his boxers.

I lay on the bed, every inch of my naked flesh vulnerable to his overwhelming hunger.

Jacob slid back into the bed, pulled me into his embrace and seized my lips. "I want nothing more than to be buried in your sweetness again," he said, rubbing his finger against my throbbing clit.

"I want you buried inside of me, too."

Taking in his kingly physique always caused me to forget anything wrong in my world. His strong jawline, broad shoulders, toned abs, and thighs were sights to behold. I scooted to the center of the massive bed and opened my legs wide enough to accept him.

He crept on top of me and pushed my legs back further with his capable arms.

"Oh!" I screamed when he entered me with precision, ripping open the protective fibers of my canal without warning.

"Shit, you're always so fucking tight," he growled as if he were surprised that my body could give way to the pressure of his size while gripping his heavenly girth for dear life. Within seconds, he possessed me with slow and deliberate strokes.

I quivered beneath him on every thrust, with what seemed to be a constant, streaming orgasm. The state of being where nothing mattered but our connection overtook me.

*Good grief, I am all his. No matter what. No matter...no...*

"Oh shit, Jacob. You feel so good. What are you doing to me, Jacob?" I called his name repeatedly, managing to ask a question between the jerking and trembling that, once again, had rapt my body with more pleasure than any one woman should endure in a lifetime.

He sucked my dark, pebbled nipple into his mouth. His suction against my tender breast caused me to violently shudder while releasing the fiercest orgasm. My thick cream covered his big cock, and spilled over onto the bed. A pool of my juices built underneath us as he bucked relentlessly inside me. My vaginal muscles entrapped and freed him repeatedly, pulling every bit of his cum out of his balls and into my thirsty canal.

"Oh, sweetheart, I'm giving my babies to you! I want you to have them all," he growled against my ear as he held me in place so I could receive all he had to give.

"*Jacob*," I moaned his name in pleasure, too weak to scream any louder. I watched his body move in a wonderful form. He was insanely sexy and I loved him to no end.

When my husband retracted from me, I immediately wanted him back inside, raging through me with full passion. I turned to my side with a smile on my face. I lay awake for a few minutes, wondering if it was a good time to tell him about our child growing inside me.

Every time we made love in the past few months, he'd declared how much he wanted us to get pregnant. The news would make him happy, but something inside me wouldn't bring me to discuss what should have been happy news for us both.

Closing my eyes, I decided to wait until he revealed why he had brought me to Atlanta. Jacob spooned me from behind, and it wasn't long before we were both fast asleep.

## Chapter Five

## Destiny

When I woke up the next morning, Jacob's side of the bed was empty. I pulled my aching body up to read the note left on his pillow.

*"I'm going to the Atlanta office for a few meetings, and I'll be back by noon. Then, we will talk...."*

Since our looming conversation had been postponed for a few more hours, I decided to use this time to take the kids to Montie's office. He would be pleasantly surprised to see them while we're in town, especially after he missed Junior's big win in Florida's all-state championship. Jacob had pulled some strings to get him on the team as a walk-on, and the coach accepted him because Junior was competitive and had already been playing little league soccer in Atlanta. And well, it might have had something to do with Jacob's generous donation to the team's travel fund. No kid on that team would have to pay to travel for at least the next couple of years.

I grabbed my cell and called Shalonda to see if I could somehow schedule a few hours of Montie's time. He blew up on me when I told him about Junior's game at the last minute. He wouldn't understand that this visit was also impromptu for me. He didn't like surprises, so he would be ticked if we just showed up when he had important meetings scheduled at the same time. Thankfully, Shalanda saw a way to clear up half of Montie's day without putting him at any inconvenience.

"I'll just have his earlier meeting come in at 1 p.m. That should be no problem," she said. "It's a feedback follow-up anyway."

"Are you sure he won't be chewing the skin off my head and reattaching it to my skull after he's gotten over his frustrations?" I asked, laughing slightly but serious as a heart attack. I didn't want any beef with Montie, which seemed to be all he was giving me as of late.

"No, Destiny. That won't be a problem. He'll be so happy to see Junior and Montana; hell, I will too. So what if he gets pissy about the surprise of it all? Can't wait to see my babies, and if you have any problem with Montie, tell him I okayed his schedule change weeks ago. Little white lies don't hurt anybody," she said and laughed.

"I don't think it'll come to that, but thanks for covering for me anyway," I laughed. "The kids are going to be so excited! Thank you so much. We'll see you in a little while."

Next, I called Lynetta.

"Good morning, Mrs. Turner. Is there anything I can do for you?" she asked in a perky voice.

"Good morning, Lynetta. Are the kids dressed? I'm about to take them to see their father since Jacob won't be coming back until noon."

"Yes, ma'am. What time would you like for us to meet you?" They were one floor down in a presidential suite.

"Come up to the penthouse in thirty minutes, but don't give them breakfast. I'm surprising them and their father with a breakfast meeting. Also, don't tell them where we're going. It's a surprise. Have the car come and get us by 7:45. I should be ready by then."

"Yes, ma'am."

I disconnected the call, went into the bathroom, and turned on the shower. I slipped out of Jacob's night robe and held my hand out to test the water. It was steaming hot, just how I liked it. I couldn't wait to step in and just clear my head for a little while.

As one foot landed in the shower, my phone rang. I picked it up from the bathroom counter and answered. "Hello."

"Good morning, my beautiful wife," Jacob's deep, soothing voice resounded through my phone's speaker.

I smiled. "Good morning, Jacob."

"Are you going somewhere?"

*Those security guys are such rats.*

"Yes, and I know your security team already called to let you know I asked them to pull the car around. Is that why you're calling?"

"Yes, they did call. Where to?"

"If you must know, Mr. Turner. I'm taking Junior and Montana to see their father."

45

"Okay, that's a good thing. And, yes, I must always know where my wife is. That's why I pay people good money to ensure you're safe. I also want to wish you a great day before I get caught up in the meeting I called with my team."

"Oh, thanks, Jacob. I hope everything is okay."

"It is now that I have talked to you. I just have to cover some ground with the Atlanta team since I'm here. Nothing to worry about, beautiful. Enjoy your morning, and I know the kids will enjoy visiting Montie. I'll see you very soon. I still plan to be out of here by noon."

"Okay, have a good meeting."

"Thanks, beautiful."

An eerie feeling that something bad was about to happen washed over me after I hung up. I shook those negative thoughts and stepped under the piping hot water spray. After a relaxing shower and a quick pampering, I dressed in a pink romper and matching pink heels with a pink bow. I wore my hair in an array of natural curls. I applied a coat of natural tone makeup and soft pink gloss. Not long after I put on my earrings, there was a knock at the door.

"Just a second," I said as I came out of the bathroom and into the hall leading to the doorway.

"Hey, Mama!" Junior ran into the room as soon as the door opened. He rushed past me and into the suite. "Where's Pops?" he asked when he didn't find Jacob.

"Mama!" Montana's tiny voice echoed as she stood at my knee, tugging on my pants to be picked up.

Hoisting Montana on my hip, I picked up my purse. "Jacob had to go to work this morning, Junior."

"Awe, man! I thought we were on vacation," my little man pouted.

"Well, this is kind of a mini-vacation. Do you guys want to see your father?"

"Yeah! Yay!" they both yelled in excitement.

"This morning, they asked me what city we were in. When I told them we were in Atlanta, they started talking about going to see their father," Lynetta inserted with a smile as she clasped her hands together, joining Junior and Montana's excitement.

"And Montie will be equally excited when we surprise him," I said.

"Mrs. Destiny, I packed some necessities they might need while we're out, and the car is waiting for us in the loop."

"Well, let's get going then," I said, happy to reunite my children with their father. Montie deserved all the time he could spend with them. He had always been an excellent father, and I couldn't imagine how he felt with them living so far away.

My security guard, Tallen, stood by the elevator and rode down with us to the car when we walked out into the hallway. Henry hopped out of a black Lincoln and opened the door for us to enter his vehicle. Our motorcade drove away, consisting of a black Denali in the back of us and another Denali in the front.

## Chapter Six

## Destiny

### *Never Can Say Goodbye*

"Heeyy, Destiny!" Montie's long-time dedicated secretary and friend, Shalanda, jumped from her chair and ran around her desk to hug my neck.

She had been a loyal worker for Montie since he began his firm. Shalanda was always polite and respectful toward me and had long ago adopted our children as her own. She hugged Junior and Montana so tight before letting them go.

"Oh, my god. You guys are growing up too fast. I need you both to stop it right now, so Auntie Shalanda can have time to spend with you while you're still babies," she pronounced.

Montana looked at Junior with a wide-eyed 'what did we do wrong' look, and he giggled at her.

"We can't stop growing up. I'm going to turn seven soon, and I can't wait," said Junior.

"I'm three," Montana added.

Shalanda reached into the bowl on her desk and pulled out two suckers. "Oh, my, my, my. Well, if you can't stop getting older, I guess that's too bad. I won't be able to give you suckers once you get too old."

Junior thought it over. "I think I can stay six a little while longer."

"And I can be three," Montana chimed in reliably.

"Okay, if you will stay six and three, I'll give these to your mother and you can eat them after breakfast with your dad."

"Thank you!" they said in unison with huge grins. Junior hugged her again and Montana followed suit.

"Thanks, Shalanda," I said, taking the candy. "Is it okay if we wait in his office to surprise him?"

"Yes, that'll be fine. I'll open it for you," Shalanda said as she walked ahead of us down the hall. She stopped in front of Montie's office door and opened it.

The kids and I went in and sat on his sofa, waiting. About thirty minutes later, the doorknob turned and Montie entered the room. He strode in with his eyes trained on his computer. Our children sprang alive from his leather sofa.

"Surprise. Surprise, daddy, surprise!" Junior ran over to Montie, holding his trophy out ahead of him. Lynetta had been thoughtful enough to pack it in his bag when she found out we were coming to Atlanta. "Look, daddy, look what I won."

Montie was in complete shocking seeing us in his office. "I see it, Son, and I'm so proud of you."

"Daddy, daddy, but my team won the all-state trophy, and we all got one to take home." Junior had talked to his father on the phone, but he still spoke to him like he was breaking the news about his win.

"I know you won, Son. And your mother sent me the awesome video of you scoring the game point. It was remarkable," Montie said, peering at me with mixed emotions that I understood so well. It was amazing that we weren't married but still spoke without speaking. I understood the hurt and pride flowing through him at once. "Give me a pound," Montie touched knuckles with Junior.

Junior jumped into Montie's arms and hugged him tightly. Euphoria filled every corner of my body as I watched them interact. This was why I fell in love with Montie in the first place. He was so compassionate.

"I'm so, so proud of you, son. I'm glad you won, but sorry I couldn't be there. I'll be there next time, and that's a promise." Montie shot me a look that said, 'because your mother will make sure that I'm there,' and I silently concurred.

"It's okay, dad." Junior hugged his father again, and my heart swelled with as much love as I thought it could take. Watching my children interact with their father had tears leaking from my eyes and down my cheek after such a long hiatus. Montie bestowed a fatherly love on our two babies that could be unmatched by any man other than their biological father.

"Thanks for coming," he mouthed to me.

"You're welcome," I replied when it should have been me thanking him for allowing the rift that he suffered from us moving to Miami.

"Had I known you guys were coming, I would have planned for a breakfast date," Montie said, breaking into my thoughts. "I need to check my calendar quick and make sure I'm free," he said, smooching Montana's cheek and telling her how much he missed her.

"Montie, that won't be necessary. I planned everything with Shalanda like you told me to do when we talked. We're your first meeting for today, and she gave us a two-hour slot, so we can still go for breakfast," I said.

"Oh, so I see now that Shalanda is just as sneaky as you are," Montie said, grinning. He sat down on his sofa with his children for a while before heading out to IHOP for a late breakfast.

Over breakfast, Montie didn't mention any of his frustrations, the driving distance between us, or how Jacob and I were raising our children. That gave me comfort enough to let my guard down with him. It felt like I had my old friend back before we got married. I relaxed and just enjoyed spending time with him and our children because the children were what it was all about.

However, he slammed me when we arrived back at his office, security detail, and Lynetta in tow (waiting in the car).

"It would've been nice if you guys stayed in Atlanta, Destiny."

"Yeah, that would have been nice. If we had stayed here, you would be more in our children's lives, and I wouldn't be in the same city as his ex." I looked away from him and sighed. "Justine is like this ever-present figure that I can't get rid of," I continued. "She comes up in discussion when his mother is around. Jacob makes it clear that he doesn't want her around us, but his mother has an attachment to her and it's excruciating for me to be around her. I'm getting to the point where I just want to move back to Atlanta, Montie."

Montie had a gleam of hope in his eyes.

I smiled and continued, "I'm tired of the entire charade of looking over my shoulder for the woman that has an invite to my in-law's home. I told Jacob that I'm uncomfortable. He's been more subdued about her, like there is something more to them than before. He told me you ended up going out with her. How did that happen?"

I spouted off more information than I planned to. The mind is a mysterious organ because I had no intention of bringing my personal life up to Montie, much less go on and on about how I feel like something is going on with her and Jacob. I was divulging too much and asking too much of Montie...again.

"Oh, Jacob told you that?" he asked and sucked in a deep breath as he stared straight through me as if he had seen a ghost standing behind me.

"Yeah, Jacob said you and Justine hooked up when you were in Miami. Is she the reason you didn't come to the wedding?" I inquired.

The furrowing lines on his forehead forewarned me that Montie was about to go completely T-Rex up in here, but I didn't cross any lines with him. He was the one that slept with the very woman who attacked me. I asked him about it, so why did he look like he was about to rip the paint off the walls?

"No, I just didn't want to be at your wedding, Destiny," he said with a look that told me he didn't want to be there because he was still in love with me at the time. "But did Jacob also tell you that he slept with Justine in your new house?" he added through tightened lips. "Damn," weakly dripped from his throat, and he stared at me in horror. He hadn't meant to let that black cat out of the bag, but there was no putting it back in now.

I leaped from the sofa. He extended his arm for me, and I jerked out of his reach. A deafening pain shot through my stomach, causing me to double over. Tears sprang from my eyes like a waterfall. All that could escape my lips from that point on was, "I knew it...I knew it...I knew...it." Any other thoughts were frozen with the news that my loving, caring, devoted husband was an all-out fraud.

Montana ran to my side.

I picked up my daughter and stormed toward the door.

"Mama, is something wrong with the baby?" Montana shared the news she overheard me telling my mother on the ride over to Montie's office. I was pregnant with the new heir to the Turner Enterprise. An enterprise I didn't want one red cent or even acknowledgment from now.

"Are you pregnant, Destiny?" Montie asked.

Another cry squealed from me, stopping me in my tracks as I reached the door. At that very spot in Montie's office, Jacob's betrayal sank into my soul and took me to an all-time low.

I swiped away my tears and held back the emotions building behind my lids for my children's sake.

"Say goodbye to your father," I whispered to Junior and Montana.

Montie apologized to me profusely and held me in his arms, friend-to-friend. I held onto his familiar caress. I needed it more than anything at that moment.

A woman walked through the door carrying a large bag of takeout and wearing a huge smile that instantly faded when she saw me.

"Hey ba—bee..." she sang, her words waning as she stepped into the solemn room.

My eyes crashed into hers and flew to Montie's.

He stepped back from me, held my hand, and squeezed it lightly. Then, he went over to greet the woman with a welcoming kiss.

I understood the loving look he bestowed upon her. I'd lost Montie completely after choosing Jacob, who cheated on me and tried to hide it. This lady had filled the void that I left wide open. She was someone special to Montie. I could tell by how he kept her protectively at his side that he had no intention of ever letting her go. He once felt that way about me, and I let him go—what a dirty brush with karma.

"I'll wait in the lobby." I bolted from the room, whimpering as I trailed up the hallway. An emotional wrecking ball, I frantically dialed Jacob to hear his side of the story.

After explaining to him what Montie had just told me, "I thought she was you, Destiny," was his sorry excuse. "I knew she was ruthless, but this is horrible. She played a dirty trick on me. I have had to live with my actions since that horrible day. I would have told you before now, but I couldn't find it in myself to tell you that I could be so stupid to make a mistake like that. But we don't have to worry about her anymore."

I lit into him when he admitted to sleeping with Justine. "I'm not worried about her anymore or you. You let her win, Jacob. How could you sleep with her of all fucking people?"

"I never would have touched her in my right mind. Listen, I don't think we should discuss this over the phone. I'm in the car now. I'm coming over to get you," he said.

"Just let me go, Jacob. This has caused too much damage already."

"Baby, we don't have to worry about her playing any more horrible tricks on us. My father just told me that she's been locked up for Rick's murder," Jacob said, adding the reason he brought me to Atlanta. "That's why I wanted to come here, back to where we started, because I knew you would be upset with me once I told you the truth. My dream is to never see a frown on your face. I couldn't bear the thought of me being the reason for you being hurt."

"Well, you have failed, Jacob," I said, ending our call.

Montie approached me, trying to apologize for his slip up. I couldn't hold back the tears any longer. I stormed out of his office onto the curb, where I stood crying senselessly.

Seeing my distress, Lynetta got out of the back of the second car and ran over to my side. "Mrs. Destiny, what is the matter?" she asked.

"Just take Montana and Junior with you."

"No, Mama, I want to stay with you," Junior asserted.

"Me stay too," Montana added. "Gotta be with you, mommy."

"No, I'm fine." I faked a smile. "Go ahead with Lynetta and she'll take you for ice cream," I said.

Lynetta got into one of the unmarked Lincolns parked by the door and I got into the other. I told Henry to take me back to the airport.

"Mrs. Turner, should I call Mr. Turner and tell him you'll be departing Atlanta."

"No, that won't be necessary. Just take me to the airport, please!"

"Yes, ma'am," he said and tilted his hat.

My cell phone rang and it was Jacob.

I answered, yelling, "Listen, just give me some time to process that you slept with the same bitch that's tried to kill me, disrespected me many times, and killed her ex-boyfriend."

Henry's eyes turned the size of quarters as he looked through the rear-view mirror after hearing the bombshells dropping.

Jacob's unusual silence in response to such a damning statement demoralized me. When he finally spoke up, he said, "It happened, but I can't express enough to you that it's not what you think, Destiny. I never would knowingly betray you for her. I'm returning to the hotel, and we can talk when I get there."

"You want to know the funny thing, Jacob? I knew in my heart she wasn't spewing lies this time. The way she described every detail of our home, and then Montie confirming that you slept with her—"

"I thought she was you, baby."

"The nerve of you to tell me that you don't know her pussy from mine! Fuck you forever, Jacob. And it's good that we haven't been married that long because I want out."

His voice deflated, "You don't mean any of what you said."

"Oh, but I do. I mean it, and I mean it more than I've ever meant anything in my life. Montie was right about you. I never should have married you."

"That right there is our problem. Too many people have been involved in our relationship. Montie and Justine have been thorns in our side the whole time. We were never in this relationship alone. We've had too many influences, and that's why we haven't been able to have an authentic relationship."

"Montie is not *involved* in our relationship. He's my children's father who just so happened to advise me on something he saw in you when he met you, which obviously turned out to be true."

"He did more than fucking advise you if you need to be reminded, Destiny."

"Funny, I told you about Montie and me getting together that night because I thought you left me, Jacob. It wasn't because I just wanted a quick lay."

"It still happened, and you weren't confused about what was going on. You knew you were letting him have something that belonged to me while holding my heart in the palm of your hand," Jacob relayed, his voice rapt with hurtful undertones.

"I explained my moment of weakness with Montie in as much detail as you wanted me to, and you forgave me. But you just skimmed over the detail *you* screwed Justine in the house you bought me as a wedding gift, the house you had to announce to the whole city through the press that you had built for our life together. What a gift?! Defiled with another woman's juices. Ha!"

"I know how this looks, but you're jumping to conclusions that you shouldn't be. Since I didn't tell you about the Justine incident upfront, like I should have, I'm going to let that part go."

"You have no choice but to let it and me go."

"Under no circumstance am I letting you go. You are my wife and I would never knowingly do anything to jeopardize that. I will spend every day of the rest of my life proving to you that I fucked up, but I'm not fucked up. I thought I was making love to my wife. I nearly choked the life out of Justine when the lights came on and I realized that she wasn't you."

"Well, it's just pretty disappointing to know that you don't know my body from the next woman. That says a lot about where we are. When I married you, I said I didn't want to go through another divorce, and sadly, that's exactly where I'm headed. I can't believe this shit," I yelled.

"Destiny, I'm not letting you go."

Henry pulled into the hotel's loop, where Jacob was pacing along the front door path.

I glared at Henry, who shrugged. "Mr. Turner texted me and asked me to bring you here," he said over his shoulder. He didn't have the nerve to look at me when he made that announcement.

I huffed and stepped out of the limo. Jacob's arms wrapped around my waist and he pulled me into his chest.

"I won't let this break us. It can't," he said with his face nuzzled against my neck.

"It has. It did. We are broken forever after this." I tried to pull out of his strong, unrelenting hold.

"You must not forget that our love is stronger than Justine's tricks. She has tried her best to ruin us the entire time I have known you. This is just another one of her schemes." A couple stopped in front of us and Jacob sidestepped so he could allow them into the building. However, he didn't let me go. "I don't want to talk about this out here," he said, grabbing my hand into his before I could get an inch away from him.

"I'm done talking, Jacob."

"Let's go to our room."

"*Your* room. And if you need to be told in your room that it's over, fine with me." I walked ahead of him and onto the elevator.

"She snuck into our home when the power was out. I was half asleep and disoriented."

"Oh yeah. When was this magical night you caught dementia and fucked the shit out of Justine?"

"That's not fair. But it was the night the power went out in the entire city, and you were out with Tasha, and I couldn't get a hold of you. I had been worried sick about you being out in the weather, but I talked myself into resting, telling myself that you were with Tasha, so you would be fine. I was so happy when I sat up on the lounger after that nap and saw you walk into the room wearing your red negligee."

"Oh my God, how could you not know it wasn't me! You let her do this to us again."

"She wore your gown to disguise herself. She wore your perfume. She wouldn't let me touch her, so I thought you were trying something different."

He stepped close to me and I slapped him with all the dragon-fire burning through my spirit. "She's a white woman Jacob and I'm black. That shit sounds ridiculous! Don't you dare treat me like I'm an idiot."

"I know it sounds crazy, but it's the truth. When I went to flip the switch to see if the light was working, you—well, she halted me by placing a finger on my lip. It was pitch black in there. I couldn't see my hand in front of my face. And then...then we made love in the pitch-dark room. I thought she was you, baby. She didn't say anything...she just...the bitch tricked me!"

I slinked against the wall, barely able to think or feel, much less look at him. He wrapped his arms around me to prop me up. I wiggled to get away from his touch. I didn't want him near me, but he would not let me break free.

"You can't hold me like this forever. At some point, I will get free and leave you. I will never forgive you for sleeping with her or keeping this secret, knowing what she has done to me. And you just went through with our wedding like nothing ever happened. Now, I have guards around me because she thinks you are hers."

"Baby, I didn't tell you because I didn't want to see this pain-filled look in your eyes. Seeing it not only breaks you but also me, and we are stronger than that."

"You're damned right; this broke us. How could you not know her body from mine?" I pressed the point of him not appreciating me as intimately as I thought he did. It made me feel cheap like I came a dime a dozen, and the feeling was nauseating.

"Ugh!" Jacob roared his outrage.

The elevator doors popped open to the floor he rented out for us. I stormed out into the hallway, and he opened the door to the penthouse. His hand came crashing down on the wall.

"I'm livid for not knowing how to answer your question. I don't know how she pulled it off, but I remember feeling woozy from my nap that day. I don't know if I thought she was you because I was half asleep and it was so dark. She's your height and weight, and I thought it was you the whole time. God knows that's the truth. Not a day has gone back that I haven't wished I could take it back."

"But you can't take it back, can you? You slept with the very woman who has spent the last year trying to kill me. Congratulations." I pushed his chest. "I can't do this right now." I ran to the bathroom, so he wouldn't see my tears fall.

Jacob blocked me from closing myself in the bathroom. "Don't lock me out. Please, babe, don't block me out."

"I don't have anything further to say, Jacob. Maybe this wasn't meant to be with everything done on both of our accounts."

"Don't do this," he said.

"I need to use the bathroom in private. Can I do that, please?"

He stepped away, allowing me to close the door.

Thankful for the time to wallow in my pain alone, I began to whimper.

"Baby, please, let me in," Jacob pled.

Whimpers turned into weeping cries as I turned on the water in the sink to splash my face. "I can't believe this is happening!" I said and cried some more. "Why, Jacob, why?" I wailed as the bathroom door came crashing open.

And Jacob was all over me. He forcibly turned me to face him, and his lips crashed into mine.

At first, I resisted him with ardent fervor, pushing and swatting at him with all the strength in my body. I didn't want him near me. I didn't want him touching me. Hugging me. Consoling me. None of it.

"Get away from me," never met the sound barrier with coherence as he muzzled my demands with his overbearing lips.

"No...never. I'm never letting you go. I love you."

"I hate you! I'm pregnant with your child, and you're sleeping with my enemy," I murmured against his lips that halted.

"You're pregnant with my child?" He looked into my eyes that gave him the answer before he assaulted my lips again. "You're having my baby," he said with so much sentimental meaning lingering in his words. "Junior and

Montana are my kids, but I'm happy as hell that you're having my first biological child. Destiny," he leaned his head back and looked at me again. "I will make this right."

I wholeheartedly hated him for putting us in this position. "How dare you get me pregnant only to let me down like this? I hate you! Our child has to be born without his father. Now, I have three children and two different fathers and no husband."

"I will always be your husband, and I will be by your side every step of the way," he said, and the smile that played with his lips incensed me more.

He pulled me closer than close. His kiss was feral, his tongue dancing against mine, trying its best to remind me that we pledged to be soul to soul, heart to heart and body to body, forever and ever.

His arousal pressed hard into my waist, and treacherous juices gushed from my vibrating lower lips. Another renegade moan slipped from me. What was my body doing to me? What kind of betrayal was this?

I hated...and loved him so much. In one swoop, Jacob picked me up into his arms.

My feet went flailing in protest of him trying to control a situation he no longer had the power to control. I screamed and kicked, "No, no! Put me down," while he repeatedly apologized from the bathroom to the bedroom.

He laid me on the bed and covered me with his tall frame. Jacob kissed me hungrily as he ground into my pelvis.

"We're having a baby," he exclaimed with that brand-new father look on his face.

A mixture of hunger and disgust traveled through my being, with disgust fading with each passing second.

He disrobed me rapidly, then himself. Once we were free of any barriers, he held my hands high above my head, firmly pressing them into the mattress. His warm lips raked over the skin of my neck. He sucked my flesh into his hungry lips, leaving his mark without bias.

"I am not yours to leave marks on anymore, Jacob."

My body betrayed my words as my flesh came alive under his weight. Reckless moans slipped from the depths of my throat up through my lips as I undulated beneath him. He trailed kisses down my neck and chest, stopping at my stomach to lovingly kiss his seed, which was growing inside me. He became relentless in his movements, circling his teeth around my nipples and biting down until I felt pain.

"I'm sorry, Destiny," he whispered, his hot breath trailing into my mouth.

As much as I hated him, I couldn't feel it at that moment.

"I don't know what you're thinking, but this isn't going to keep me, Jacob."

He spread my legs wide, mounted me and entered me with one thrust, his shaft deep inside me, punishing me for his transgressions. His lips forcibly took over my mouth as I lay helpless to the feeling of wanting my husband but not wanting him all the same. He hammered into my tender flesh, exhibiting his need for what would be his one last time. His pounding drive into my aching pussy was enough to keep me completely submissive to his plunder.

Jacob growled from deep within, and I couldn't help but think about him in our home with her. So many tears flowed from my eyes and hit the covers beneath me, wetting the bed with his senseless betrayal.

Jacob retracted from me, kissing my tears away. His breathing was ragged, but the crease lines on his forehead were ferocious. His fist slammed down into the cottony sheets beside my head. He held me in his arms as a flurry of "I'm so sorry" and "I'll never hurt you again" brushed against my earlobe.

As I dressed minutes later, I felt relieved to be released from his stronghold, at least mentally. It wasn't going to be easy to separate from him. Yet, it had to be done.

## Chapter Seven

## Destiny

Each passing day, I found it harder to forgive Jacob. I did go back to Miami with him, but after day three, I moved out of our bedroom and into the guestroom. It took some hard negotiating for Jacob to let me leave our bedroom without protesting. He didn't want me to leave our home, so he gave me space. To make things worse, three weeks after finding out that he slept with Justine, the Miami Herald printed an article with the headline, *"Convicted Murder Justine Parker Claims to be Pregnant with the Heir to the Turner Enterprise."* I immediately began shipping my belongings back to Atlanta after reading that article.

Justine had been sentenced to twenty-five years for the murder of her ex. DNA evidence and her lipstick being found on the scene were the nails in her coffin. Now, the murderous bitch was calling up news outlets, telling them she was pregnant with Jacob's baby.

"We can work this out," Jacob assured me. He stood at the door of our master bedroom closet, watching me pack. "Stay…"

"This is it for us. Tasha's on her way to take us to the airport." I slammed my last suitcase shut with my mind reeling over how fast our love story had gone from everlasting to finish. There was no way I could deal with another woman's child, particularly one conceived by a woman who held me at gunpoint. His stepping out on our relationship with her would solidify our true end.

"You didn't have to get Tasha involved. I would have taken you or gotten someone to take you."

"Well, I don't need anything from you, Jacob! Not even a ride." I had settled into the lifestyle where Jacob was taking care of me, but I had to get back to the basics, where I went hard for myself without depending on a man to do anything for me. *What a wake-up call.*

Jacob's face didn't show emotion other than the darkness in his sad eyes. "I know I messed up, and it may seem beyond repair, but I need you to know that I will never give up on us. We will be together again by some stroke of good luck or good karma. We weren't built to fail, so I'll take this time as just a trial."

I rolled my eyes away from him. "This is hardly a trial, Jacob."

"It is, and you will see."

"Okay, riddle me this. Who will take care of Justine's baby while she's locked up for the rest of her life...you? Definitely not *me*!"

Jacob didn't have an answer to that question, and to be honest, I don't think it had yet dawned on him that Justine's child would need someone to care for it.

Yeah. We were done.

If he was the father, he would be the next person to care for the child. He wasn't the kind of man to neglect his responsibilities, so I could only imagine him bringing her child home from prison and expecting me to be there for him. I wasn't prepared for this, and neither did I think I was capable of preparing for it. I was three months pregnant, making Justine's supposed baby one month older than mine by pregnancy dates.

"All I know is that I love you...*you*, and the baby growing in your stomach. I don't care anything about Justine."

"But her baby, Jacob."

"I love *you*."

"Love isn't supposed to make you hurt like hell. I'm supposed to be happy, and I'm not. I can't be with you until I figure out how to deal with everything happening."

"Don't leave me. Do you want me to get on my knees and beg you because I will?" He dropped to his knees and looked up at me with pleading eyes. "Baby, don't go, please."

"No amount of begging will keep me here." The doorbell rang and I walked toward the door. "That's Tasha."

Jacob rushed to follow me to the door. He caught me from behind and took my suitcase from my hand. "I'll carry this for you. I don't want you to hurt the baby."

"Thanks." I turned and walked away from the man who had a sudden interest in being concerned about our family. "Junior, Montana! Come on, we're about to leave now," I said as I stopped by their rooms.

They ran out ahead of me and downstairs to meet Tasha.

At the top of the staircase, Jacob touched my arm.

"What?"

"This is only temporary. I'm coming for my family as soon as I can prove that I never meant to hurt you."

I started to walk down the stairs, then rushed to the bottom, where Tasha stood boring holes through Jacob with fire and brimstone in her chocolate brown eyes.

Upon making eye contact with me, Tasha grabbed the kids' hands and said, "Come on to the car with me."

The kids broke free, ran over to hug Jacob's leg, and told him goodbye before galloping behind Tasha to the car.

I turned to face Jacob. I took one last look around the house that was almost mine. "For what it's worth, I still love you and always will, but Justine being pregnant with your child is more than I can deal with, now or at any time in the future." And I couldn't imagine helping Jacob raise her child, which would only be a month or two older than mine. "So, this is goodbye."

"For now," he said simply.

I reached out for my bag, but he refused to give it to me, insisting on taking it to the car. I shrugged and went and sat in the car. As far as I was concerned, it would be the last thing he ever did for me.

## Chapter Eight

## Jacob

### Understanding is What I Need...

I woke up in the dead of night to crickets chirping, a melodic blend with the occasional frog croaking through my open window. I reached for Destiny every night since she'd been gone. Her side of the bed was cold, and my hand came down to rest on her empty pillow. Not only was she absent from my bed, but she was also no longer in the guestroom. At least when she stayed in the guestroom, I could go stand by the door and feel her energy wafting through the air. Her essence vibrated through me in the spiritual sense, and that was enough for me. But with her gone and hurt by my actions, I was slowly going insane.

I slid into my suede slippers and trekked along the mahogany wood of my lengthy, third-floor hallway. I peeked inside Junior and Montana's empty rooms, and my plight became excruciatingly real. My family was gone.

After staying at the Marriott Atlanta for a week, I flew back to Miami hours ago. I tried to reach Destiny on a deep level to get her to remember me, the man she married. I wanted her to think about if she felt I would cheat and risk losing her. I needed to get her to understand what happened from my standpoint, but she wasn't listening to me.

In my mind, I kept thinking that if I didn't know I was sleeping with Justine, technically, I didn't sleep with her. Justine's bombshell about her baby beat my case to smithereens.

Destiny tuned me out. If she heard me, she didn't understand how it could happen the way I said it did. She moved back into her old house that, to my chagrin, hadn't sold on the market yet. She would barely let me through the door until I threatened to knock it down. I would never go that far, but I needed to get her attention.

*Give me time Jacob.*

*Let me go, Jacob.*

*This is it, Jacob.*

She kept asking me to give her time and let her go. I refused to do either. And this definitely wasn't it for us. I dreaded being separated from her, and since she told me about my baby growing in her womb, that dread went up exponentially. Her having part of me inside her was more reason I could never just let her go like she wanted me to. She was mine, the baby was mine, and there was nothing no one could do to change that.

The only reason I made the trip back to Miami without my family was to confront the people who meddled in my marriage and caused Destiny and me to come to this heart-wrenching halt.

There were some bad actors from day one. If it weren't for them needing to be addressed, I would have been in Atlanta groveling like a bitch, trying to prove to Destiny that she was the only woman for me, always had been, and always would be.

My first stop was at my mother's house after getting up and dressed. I went into the garage and hopped in my SUV. I had given Henry the day off.

Thirty minutes later, I pulled up to Mom's freshly built village-style estate. Construction was still happening on one part of the mansion, but the landscaping on the front yard was complete, with Miami palms strategically sculpting the driveway. She had spared no expense in building a home just as exquisite as the one my grandparents passed down to Dad, the one she had been exiled from because of her inability to be a compassionate, loving woman.

I parked my Lincoln in front of the walkway to the front door, hopped out, and sighed. No man ever wants to have the kind of conversation I was about to have with my mother, but it was going down. I strolled to the door and rang the bell.

Surprisingly, it took Mom three minutes, which gave me plenty of time to think about how to broach the conversation with her.

"Why if it isn't my—"

"She left. Are you happy?" I cut her off.

"Son..." she finished her statement and then asked, "Who left?"

"Destiny, she left me, and she won't be coming back, thanks to your and Justine's constant games that you played. Now, the papers are printing that Justine is pregnant with my child, which is probably just another game she's playing." I glared at my mother. "Did you know about this?"

"No, I read about it at the same time as you probably did, Jacob. And wait a minute. You're coming in here hurling accusations. Why on earth would I be happy that your wife left you, Son?" she asked, but before I could answer, she said, "Poor girl never knew what she had in the first place. If Justine hadn't gone crazy and killed that man, she would've been the perfect wife for you, whether she played games or not."

"You're wrong for defending Justine's bullshit, Mom. Do you even hear what you are saying? Justine never was the woman for me. Destiny is. I didn't know love until I met her. It's just a shame that you would want me to be with a murderer, just because you and your friend arranged for us to be together when we were kids, instead of Destiny."

"I never said that."

"But, you did say it."

"Son, I just wanted what was best for you."

"Bullshit, and you know it! Rick would still be alive if you had not played with Justine's marriage."

Mom's eyes bucked wide and her jaws tightened with her lips in a straight line across her face. "You don't know what you're talking about, Jacob!"

75

"Oh, but I do know because I went by and talked with his wife, and she told me all about what you did to interfere in Justine and Rick's engagement, including paying her money to quit the guy she was with and try to get Rick back. You knew that since she and Rick already had children he would be willing to reconcile. He didn't want to leave Justine, but you and Martha kept interfering until he was persuaded to return to his family and leave Justine at the altar. Do you know that man would probably still be alive, and Justine wouldn't be facing hard time if you had not meddled in their relationship? Instead, she would probably be happily married."

"Watch how you are talking to me, Jacob. I'm still your mother."

"Only a sorry excuse of a mother would participate in a scheme to tear two people who love each other apart. Then, you dishonor my wife while propping up the woman you drove looney by your interference. Now, Justine's life is ruined, and Rick's is gone. That hurts me deeply, but what hurts even more is that the mother of *my child,* and your grandchild, is distraught because you kept allegiance to Justine after she attacked her."

"Destiny is pregnant, too?" Mom asked in classic fashion. She was more concerned with who would be the heir of Turner than all her dirty shenanigans that had ruined so many lives.

"Yes, she is pregnant with the only rightful heir of Turner Enterprises. If Justine tries to drag me into a paternity battle, I will have no recourse than to expose her for the sperm stealer she is."

"If her child is yours, then he or she will be an heir. We will take care of her baby and love it because we care for ours, plain and simple."

"Yeah, like you have taken care of me, Mom? No, thanks."

"What exactly are you trying to say?" she asked incredulously.

"You spend too much time caught up with what other people think, you always have, and you never took the time to see what we thought about you or us. You just care about appearances. That is probably why you came to our wedding and made a big show of your apology. But that appearance you imagined for our family is over. Dad's gone, and soon I'll be gone too," I said, certain she wasn't going to change her ways. I wasn't about to change my worldview either, which meant there was no way for us to go but in separate directions.

I had to look out for what was important to me and stop trying to feed plants that were dead at the root. That's a hard pill to swallow about my flesh and blood, my mother, the first woman I ever loved, but when you know better, you do better.

Mom's love didn't flow like a fluid river both ways, and I would die of thirst waiting to be nourished by it. I refused to die. My river was flowing in Atlanta. With my seed growing in the woman I loved, there was a waterfall of love I'd miss out on if I kept holding on to the past.

I didn't have anything holding me in Miami. With Destiny gone, Atlanta was the only place I wanted to be.

"You know I really loved your father," Mom cut into my thoughts.

"You had an odd way of showing it, Mom."

"I may not have shown it the right way. I'm different from others, but it doesn't mean I don't have love in me, Son. Your father was the love of my life. I'll never find anyone else quite like John."

"Dad is a good man," I agreed. "But his heart was someplace else, Mom. The last thing a man wants is to live his life knowing that his heart is in another household. It hurts deep and is something the wrong woman can never repair."

Mom gasped as hurt filled her hardened features. "I understand that better than you think I do. I only brought up your father to tell you I love you, too. I just love in my own way."

I didn't care about her differences in love. She never cared about how badly I'd be hurt by her constant backing of Justine's mess. She didn't care enough to respect my heart, which beat inside Destiny's chest. Therefore, I was done with it all. It was time for me to move on with my mind and conscious clear of people I once loved to no end but who had disregarded and disrespected my love life.

"Jacob," she continued, sitting on the sofa and folding her arms around her knees. She looked out at the sunset through her wall-sized open window. "Maybe I pulled so hard for Justine because I knew how she felt."

"So, you sympathized with her more than you did your own son?" I asked.

"Your father loved that woman," she ignored my question and continued. "I always knew about her and the way he felt about her. Sometimes, he would say her name in his sleep in the most endearing way. He would also smile at the dinner table as he looked through me. He often thought of her, imagining she was there with him instead of me. The story about how he fell in love and ended up being forced to break up was no secret to the locals back in the day. I filled in time and space for him, like Justine was filling in a time and place for you until you met the right one. The one that *set your soul on fire*, like John said about Clara."

"What you're telling me is that you felt sorry for Justine because she was a younger version of you?" I asked for clarity.

"Yeah, Son. I know it wasn't right, but that's how I felt."

"Well, Justine did something that I may be unable to repair. Honestly, I don't know if I can return from this."

"So what if you slept with her? She told me the day after it happened about you guys making love in your home," Mom said, waving her hand dismissively while speaking in a tone that minimized Justine's actions. "The poor girl came over

79

here, crying her eyes out, saying that you choked her after you had sex with her and put her out of your house."

"That's because she was an intruder."

"Oh, Son, you can't help the feelings you still have for Justine. I know they are there. Justine knows they are there. You are the only one denying it while trying to bolster up Destiny, who must not have been satisfying your needs. If she were, then there would have been no way for Justine to seduce you."

I punched my right fist into my left hand and roared to release the steam growing inside of me and about to bubble over. "You don't know anything about me, and you never have. I had no idea I was 'making out' with Justine. It was pitch black in my house, and she pretended to be Destiny."

"That's not the way she described it to me, but—"

"Come on now. Wouldn't you agree her credibility is shot now that she's facing prison time for being a soulless murderer?" I wasn't entirely sure why I was still trying to reason with her.

"She's still our Justie, Jacob."

"No, she's your Justie. She isn't anything to me. She turned into a monster, which apparently happens when people meddle in places they shouldn't. If I lose Destiny for good after all this is said and done, I will lose it too, Mom."

"Don't say that. The Turners are not losers," she mulled over everything I just told her about Justine. Though she gave face like she was keeping it together, I could see the layers beneath her trembling. I had even more facts for her that would strengthen the wedge between our mother-son bond.

"The heir to the Turner Enterprise will be lost. I will be subjected to being a weekend father when my father and grandparents didn't do that to me. I will have muddied the Turner waters."

"Muddied the waters...you can say that again," Mom murmured underneath her breath.

"You know," my heart slammed against my chest as I growled at my egg donor and incubator. "I gave you chance after chance to be decent because you are my mother, and it took me too long to believe that I could come from someone so vile. But I should have known from the beginning that all your reconciling and asking for forgiveness was fake. I should have protected Destiny better from you and Justine."

"Jacob, you're the one that needed protection from Destiny. She came in here broke and trying to steal a small fortune by becoming your wife with no prenup contract, and now she has a baby. Look at the writing on the wall. Can't you see that she set herself up for a nice win at your expense?"

"I want her to have every penny she wants to take from me. I'm willing to give it to her freely. No one is forcing me to give Destiny anything. I give to her because I want to. To be able to give the woman I love everything her heart desires is what the money is for."

"Aw, you and your father are so much alike," she sprang to her feet and stood in my face, barking as spittle flew

81

from her mouth. "Always thinking with your heart, your peckers, and what you think *means* something to you. You should know that what means something is family and the upkeep of our name and enterprises!"

"Being like Dad is a compliment because right now what means the most to me is to get you out of my life, so Destiny and I can start over for the final time building on solid ground with no distractions."

Mom gasped. "Distraction? Jacob, I gave you life, and you stand in my face calling me a distraction? I have never done anything but what was right for you."

It hurt to say something so damning to my mother, but it was the truth, and the truth hurts. "By disrespecting the very woman who gave me a second shot at true love, you have hurt me more than you know. I love that damn woman, Mom, and I love the baby growing inside of her with all that I am as a man. I wanted to believe that you had changed. When I thought about what got me and Destiny to this point, I realized I can't let you continue to damage my relationship or our child because you are damaged. I wish you a good life, mother, but that's why I came by today to let you know to your face that I will never be speaking to you again."

I wanted to add 'unless she gets her act together and is genuinely ready to treat Destiny like a human being that I cherish with all my heart.' But I'd watched my mother play games with people's feelings all my life. She was about status and appearances. None of that was about to change. I wasn't willing to give her any more leverage to sprinkle hate over my marriage that I was determined to keep.

"You can't mean that," Mom said as I turned the handle on her front door to leave. "You just need some time to cool down and get over your feelings for her. Then, maybe find someone who can make you happy."

"No, I know where my happiness can be found. I just hope that you spend some time finding yours." And if that is with the upscale lifestyle, she fought so hard over the years to uphold, then so be it.

With Justine locked up, my mother made me the second toxic person who was out of my life. I didn't care who would be next. I had tunnel vision to get my woman back, no matter what it took.

## Chapter Nine

## Destiny

### *Just Me and You*

I stepped outside to get the morning paper and the misty morning air greeted me. Fury raged inside my heart at the sight of Jacob sitting on my porch stairs. Yet, my heart still skipped a beat. When he stood to face me, the apologetic look on his face made it hard to hate him. I could kick my own ass for still loving that man.

He presented me with a bouquet of pink roses. "Good morning."

"Thanks, but you shouldn't have brought those here. I don't want them." I turned to walk back inside. "You shouldn't even be here."

"Wait."

"What do you want, Jacob?"

"To talk."

"Too late for that."

"Can I come in?"

"Again, what do you want, Jacob?"

"You." He clasped his hand around my arm, gently hauled me to him, and then leaned down to capture my lips.

I moved my face, and his kiss landed on my cheek. Rearing my hand back, I pushed him away from me.

He took hold of my wrists and held me steady in front of him. "We need to talk."

I yanked myself free of his hold and walked inside, leaving the door open. He shadowed me in a slow stride.

I sat down at the kitchen table. He sat down across from me. I studied every line and contour of the man who sat in my face and lied to me until the day we married.

"Talk Jacob! You only have a short time to say what you have to say and get out of here."

"You don't have to be so mean-spirited when talking to me. That's not you, and this is definitely not who we are to each other."

"Okay, so you came in here to be the morality police? No, thank you," I stood from my seat. "I won't sit here and be lectured about how I should respond to your actions. If that's all you have to say, you can leave now."

Anxiety ran across his face. Hurt entered his eyes. "Justine has been a problem for us from day one. I understand why you don't believe me when I say I didn't intentionally have sex with her."

"Ha, it's such bullshit," I spat.

"See, I don't get how, even if I did have sex with her, you would sit here and judge me to be a low-down, dirty cheater. I fought to get you back when you stepped out on me with Montie. I accepted you and your reasoning for giving away what was rightfully mine. I trusted you with him after you slept with him, too. I have full faith in you because I know you and your heart. You don't even know who I am."

I struggled to process his perspective. Only because he had yet to understand mine. "You started off good. Most of our problems do stem from Justine and her deception. However, what has hurt me more than anything you mentioned is that you knew you had sex with her, whether before or afterward, and you kept it a secret. And, you still would be keeping that secret had Montie not blurted it out or had Justine not revealed her baby in the newspaper," I yelled.

"You're right. I didn't want to see you hurt, but I should have told you. I don't think you understand that I would rather walk over hot coals barefoot than see you hurt."

"Well, I'm hurt, and I don't think I'll ever get over this. She's having your baby," I said in a weeping tone that upset me. I didn't want to fucking cry. I wanted to unleash the pent-up wrath I felt onto Jacob like a hurricane. Instead, I broke down right in front of him.

He quickly stood and rounded the table. His strong arms encircled me as he peppered kisses all over my head and face.

"Let me go! I don't want you to touch me. Stop kissing me." I thrashed my way out of his arms.

He somehow ended up with my hands in his. "Stop it. You're going to upset the baby."

My heart broke all over again at the mention of our innocent baby. I took deep breaths and attempted to calm down. "My baby will be fine. You just make plans to take care of Justine's."

Jacob crooked his head to the side and glared at me as if the thought of her child being his responsibility had never crossed his mind.

"You are my only concern," he said in a tone that brooked no argument.

"It's over between us," I reminded him.

"No. It's not over between us. We have years to spend together, memories to make, and love to share." His eyes bored holes into me. "What we have is real. I don't know about you, but I can't stop being real."

I took a long look at him. Too many lies had been told, and my heart was starting to wonder if trying to sort out truth from fiction was worth it.

"I want you to leave my house. We can talk another time."

"No. There's an emergency in Utah that I'm flying out to handle tomorrow. However, I'm not leaving here while you're this upset." His head dipped and we were eye to eye. "So, if you want to get rid of me, and I know you do, you'd better get that painful look off your face or talk to me, preferably both."

"You're not in control anymore. You're in my house and I talk to you on my terms!" I said.

His hazel orbs glazed over with aggravation. His lips covered mine. His tongue slid into my mouth and caressed me before I could even think to gripe.

Unwanted feelings of love and security from my husband rushed over me as he ran his hands over my back. I closed my eyes and melted into his embrace. *Damn, I may be cursed with loving this man forever. This is not fair.*

"Make love to me," he muttered against our deep and passionate kiss.

"No," I whispered back.

He urgently caught my denial between his lips.

"I don't want to fight. Make love to me, baby. I need you."

Too weak for a verbal response, I shook my head, which he steadied in between his strong hands. His kiss lulled me deeper into the fiery abyss of our love where nothing mattered but becoming one with Jacob.

"Stop it, Jacob! No." I found my strength and snapped back away from him. I held my hand up and pushed him away as hard as I could. "I don't want to make love to you," I said, while every indicator that I craved my husband was visibly evident by my pouty lips, hardened nipples, and swollen, wet nether region.

He threw his hands up in surrender.

*Finally, he respects my wishes. Thank you.*

Our erratic breaths and pounding heartbeats returned to normal. Then, I took a step forward and looked up at him. I stared into his hazel eyes for understanding.

Did he just make the wrong judgment call by not telling me about Justine, or was he being deceptive? Answering these questions would help me decide whether I could trust Jacob again. Lord knows, I wanted to.

I rested a hand on his blazer and sighed helplessly.

Jacob took that as a sign that I was too stubborn to say what I needed. His lips came crashing down onto mine. We stood in the kitchen, making out until my mind clouded in anticipation of otherworldly ecstasy. Maybe I did need to slip away from my miseries—again. If only for the duration of the fall.

He kissed me all the way from the kitchen to my bedroom. We fell onto the bed as his hands caressed my breasts. I moaned my pleasure and wrapped my arms around his neck tightly.

This moment of weakness was a mistake that would confuse us both, but he was my husband and I craved to feel something other than the contempt that had consumed me for the past three weeks.

Jacob quickly discarded my clothing and his. Our naked bodies pressed together with an intense desire to fuse. The dance between our tongues continued. His tongue would slide against mine, and a shiver would run down my spine. My tongue would cuddle his, and he would groan in delight. I ached for the moment our bodies became one.

"I will always be here for you and my baby," Jacob said as he ran his hand over my slight baby bump. "There's only me, you and our children. She is a nonfactor to me. Do you understand me?"

I didn't answer. The heartache caused by him bringing her up must have shown.

He plowed into my tender flesh, ripping me open for him.

"Just me and you, Destiny," he said, grazing his lips across mine.

"Jacob," I moaned against his lips.

He made love to me, staring into my soul, speaking to me in ways he could never express out loud. My lower lips gripped his rod as he entered and exited with loving yet forceful strokes.

After intense lovemaking, he crashed down on top of me. His hot seed gushed against my contracting vaginal walls. We lay gazing into each other's eyes, seeing past the flesh and into untold, metaphysical places I could only imagine sharing with him.

## Chapter Ten

## Destiny

"Girl, my poetry friends are still buzzing about your piece. They want to know when you're returning to spit for open mic."

"Honey, that was over a month ago. There is no way they are still talking about that poem," I said, smiling and feeling good that something I made up on a whim was still relevant in Tasha's poetry circle. I imagined I could create something even better if I put my mind to it.

"Sis, don't downplay your talent. What you spat was nice for it to be unrehearsed. Some poets have been going in there for years and can't do a piece with that much boldness that holds people's interest," Tasha assured. "And where have you been? I've been trying to call you for the last week?"

I had been back in Atlanta for a little over a month. Tasha and I talked every day for the first week, but since Jacob went to Utah, I had been using that time to get my house back in order—something he was very much against and spent many hours each day distracting me from when he was in Atlanta. "I've been getting this house together," I said.

"Oh, yeah? I forgot Jacob has been doing everything to keep you from fixing that house. I know he hates that he had an emergency in Utah. He probably left Atlanta kicking and screaming on his jet."

She laughed, and I joined in.

"Yeah, I've had three peaceful weeks with him gone. Every day, he sends me a text adding to the list of things he wants us to do when he returns. He wants us to go to Germany to see this baby specialist or to California to see that one, and for me to do water aerobics because it's good for the baby. He's using our baby to stay close to me. He acts like none of this Justine mess ever happened. He's trying to take up as much of my time as—"

"You let him," Tasha finished my sentence not quite how I would have.

"I guess, but thank God he's out of town. I haven't had to worry about him hovering over me, calling every five minutes, hand-delivering insane amounts of flowers, or camping out on my porch refusing to leave until I talk to him," I said, omitting that I gave in to him the morning before he left town.

"Whatever is going on in Utah must be terribly important for him to still be there."

"The Utah office is in crisis. He had to fire the director because he was accused of sexual misconduct, and Turner is being sued."

Tasha gasped. "I knew it had to be something on that scale. That man is determined to get you back. And I can't say I blame him. You come from a good stock of people," she gloated.

"Yeah, well, I don't see that happening." I sighed. "We're more than likely finished."

"You love him. I can hear it in your voice whenever we talk about him. What he did makes me mad as hell whenever I think about it, but I also know he loves you. I saw that in his eyes when I pulled out of his driveway with you and the kids in the car."

"Well, love doesn't keep everything together. Honesty and loyalty are just as important. And, before you go in on me, I know I did my dirt, but I had not accepted his marriage proposal and I wasn't planning for a wedding while screwing Montie. I think that's a big difference, along with the fact that I came clean with him. I put all my cards on the table and let him have the choice of whether he wanted to play the hand," I argued.

"And he chose you."

"I guess he chose us both since he was still with her and we're both pregnant at the same time," I said with pain in my tone.

"Aw, Desti. I'm torn. I was against him initially because I thought he was just a rich, white prick who wanted to take advantage of you. However, I came to like him and think of his genuine love for you. Jacob has really got me messed up with this."

"If you're messed up, then you know I'm destroyed. So, I guess the question is am I going to sit on the phone and mope about him all night or do we have something uplifting to talk about?" I asked and giggled nervously.

"Do you need me to come to Atlanta, keep you company, and help you organize your house? You shouldn't be lifting or moving heavy furniture. Please tell me you're not trying to move that furniture alone, Ms. Superwoman."

"Oh no, Montie has been helping me a lot."

"Montie?" she gasped, and I could imagine the questions running through her mind.

"Montie *and* his girlfriend, Lissa, were nice enough to offer me a hand. Montie got one of his frat brothers to move the big furniture with him, while Lissa helped me clean and reorganize the kid's room. This house was a dusty mess, but it's looking good now."

"Hold on," Tasha said and the line went silent. "I'm back. I had to go pinch myself. Did you just say Montie and his girlfriend helped you move?"

"Yeah, the kids are gone with them now to give me time to relax, but I'm up working instead."

"You've got to be shitting me. Montie...and his girlfriend...at your house?"

"You're a mess, Tasha. I'm not entertaining you either."

"I'm just saying. How did that work with the three of you being there at once? The last time I saw Montie, it was written all over his face that he was still in love with you."

"Well, I like Lissa, so everything was cool with her being here. Montie has fallen head over tail in love with her, and that's the only thing that shows on his face when she is around," I said.

"He must really like her to bring her around you. Not too long ago, his nostrils were wide open sniffing for your scent," she said in a high-pitched tone. "Now, he's bringing his new girl around. I don't know whether to be happy or ticked with him."

"Be happy for the man. I am. But I can't lie. At first, I was a little bruised when I saw them together, how much she looked like me, and how he couldn't keep his hands off her. What could I say, though? I remarried and asked him to be a part of making my marriage work by letting the kids move to Miami. He was willing to try for me, so I'm doing the same for him. Besides, it's hard for me to feel anything about Montie being with Lissa but happiness for them both. She told me about the men who hurt her in the past and how she's blessed to have Montie. At least they're in love, and I'm happy for them."

"I get it. You're happy *for them*. What about you and Jacob, though? Maybe your love story doesn't have to end where it is. If it does, Justine gets what she wanted all along."

"Tasha, give me a break with the Jacob hypothesizing. What's done is done and cannot be undone, no matter what Justine tried to do or how bad I want him."

"Listen, let me just tell you that I thought his story about Justine sneaking sex from him sounded like fuckery off the top, but the more I remember the night Miami went black I think it's damn sure possible."

"Oh, so it appears that you've drank of the Jacob Kool-Aid. You think she snuck into our house, went up into our room, slipped into my pajamas, sprayed on some of my perfume, went into his study where he was sleeping, and screwed him until she was pregnant with his child, all without him knowing until the deed was done? At no point from the time he entered her body to the time he impregnated her did he realize it was her and not me," I repeated the ignoramus story bitingly.

"It's possible," Tasha mumbled as if attempting to make herself believe the bogusness of Jacob's claim. "I mean, I'm not taking up for him, but I'm a hard sleeper. A burglar could sneak off with me in his arms and I wouldn't realize I wasn't in my bed unless my alarm went off in my pajama pocket, and I still might not wake up then."

"Don't overanalyze for him, Tasha. This happened weeks before we got married. If she tricked him, and he knew she tricked him, he had ample time to tell me about it. That way, I could have dusted her off for sneaking into my house and messing with my man. But did he do that? No. He kept it a secret and our whimsical insta-love fantasy lived on like nothing happened." I repeated the excruciating memories that prohibited me from giving my heart back to Jacob completely. Those reminders replayed in my mind every day like a sad, old-school music video where the girl with a big heart falls deep in love and gets played.

"Jacob should have told you what happened. I'm not trying to defend that point, but I can't help but feel he got duped. He's not that stupid to sleep with Justine. He's always shown her contempt and you love. It just doesn't add up."

"That's what I've been saying all along, but it's true, cousin. I just have to live with it. That's why I'm fixing my house back up—if that indicates how close Jacob is to getting me back," I said as I dropped a laundry basket down on my bed and began folding my clothes and putting them into the drawers. "Enough about me and my woes. Tell me what's going on with you. Are you still babysitting for that sexy boss of yours, Matt?" Tasha had sent me a picture of Matt to show me the man paying her enough money to buy a small community for babysitting his nephew.

"You know I'm still working for Matt. Why would I leave him? Girl, that man is going to need the sheriff to kick me out, and I'll still be holding on to the doorpost as they try to push me out the door, screaming 'no, don't fire me!'"

I laughed harder than I had in a while, imaging Tasha acting up about having to leave Matt.

"I've made more money babysitting than I have writing or any other job I have done in my life," she continued.

"Why is it that when you talk about him I get this feeling that the money isn't the only thing keeping you there?" I pressed.

"Huh?"

"Oh, now you're dumbfounded," I snickered. "You love to write and working for a high-profile magazine press is your dream job. You never even liked to be around kids before. Now, you're the best sitter on this side of the map. What's really going on?"

"That's not true. I love Junior and Montana; they're kids," Tasha said. "As far as the rest of what you said, I plead the fifth."

"You better plead because I know how you are with kids, too. Junior and Montana are the first children I have seen you not use your three-feet rule on."

"Yeah, well, maybe it was time for me to change that and let the little creatures in my space. I've found so much joy being around Cody; he's one of the brightest and kindest little boys I know. He's a lot like his uncle, too."

"You never did tell me why Matt has custody of him."

"His parents died in a car accident, leaving Matt as his custodian. His nanny got deported back to Mexico earlier this year, so Matt needed a babysitter. My friend Dana told me that Matt was looking for a sitter and set me up to meet him, since I was looking for work. Cody and I clicked the first day I went over there, and we've gotten close. It would kill me if I couldn't be there with him. He's become such a big part of my life in such a short time," Tasha relayed in a sincere tone that melted my heart.

"Whoa, sounds like two men have stolen your heart," I said.

"No, just Cody. Matt has his own life. That's why he has me babysitting Cody so much: he can go out on dates and do whatever he likes. Therefore, no matter how sexy he looks, I'm not falling for the games men like him play."

"Well, I can't say that's a bad idea."

Jacob's handsome face flashed through my mind and lingered for far too long. I wondered if I would ever think of being loved without images of his gorgeous smile tormenting my mind.

The ringing doorbell brought my attention back to the phone in my hand.

"Hold on, Tasha, someone is at the door," I said as I strolled up the hallway.

I peeked through my peephole, and lo and behold, the devil stood arrogantly on the other side. "Why is he back in town already?" I mumbled.

"Who is it, Jacob?"

"Yeah." I blew out a loud huff. "He was supposed to be in Utah for another week."

"I guess he couldn't stay away from you that long. I'll let you go talk to your husband. Remember what I said earlier."

"Oh, I will, but this won't take long. I'll call you right back." Determined not to give in to him this time, I ended the call and spoke through the door. "What do you want, Jacob?"

"Let me in. I want to talk to you."

"No, I'm busy. Call me tomorrow."

"Tomorrow? I'm not waiting that long to see you. I've been gone for three weeks already. Now, let me in. It's cold out here."

Standing at the door listening to him would only cause me to crumble. I'd probably get lost in his relentless demands, open the door to hear his velvety voice full of promises to make things right, and fall six feet under his mind-numbing kiss, as I had done before. I still had a lot to figure out on my own.

Therefore, I walked toward my bedroom with light, slow steps to finish putting my clothes back in their rightful places. I was determined to rebuild my life the best way I knew how.

## Chapter Eleven
## Jacob

### *Ex to Ex*
### *The Tables Have Turned*

After knocking at Destiny's door for the past ten minutes, I returned to my car and sat in the driver's seat. I was tired of the back and forth. Before I went to Utah, she let me in and temporarily made me the happiest man alive. She gave me what I needed most, her unrestricted love. Other days, I was reduced to sitting in the car, being her protector from the sidelines.

I didn't stake out in front of her house because I was some jealous, obsessed husband. No. I did it because I didn't want anything I could have prevented from happening to her. I had an unmarked car watching her house when I wasn't available to do it myself. I had to know she, our baby, Junior and Montana were always okay.

Settling into my seat, I turned on the radio and Dylan Scott touted off about his girl. His song made me reflect on how I got to this place where Destiny didn't consider herself *my girl*.

*"Yeah, that's my girl. In my truck, in the songs, I sing with the radio. My girl. In my heart, my soul and the air I breathe every day...."*

I reached the bridge of "My Girl" and was in full country boy singing mode when Montie's BMW pulled into my girl's driveway. My stepchildren sprinted from the car to the door. Montana wore a pretty pink dress with a headful of pretty bows. Junior wore blue slacks and a blue and white button-down collar shirt.

I scrambled to get the door open, hopped out of the car and jogged up to the door behind them. "Junior, Montana!" I screamed their names.

When they saw me, they ran over and leaped into my arms.

I snatched both of them up and hugged them tightly. I didn't want to let go. "I missed you guys so much," I said after kissing the tops of their heads.

"Miss you too," Montana said in her sweet, little voice.

"Hey, Mr. Jacob," Junior said. He was back to calling me Mr. Jacob instead of Pops. That let me down hard. At least he was still speaking to me. "I'm about to go inside with my Mama," he quickly added as he wiggled out of my embrace.

I watched Junior run up the lawn and to the front door. Montana stayed in my arms with her head rested on my chest. I rested my jaw on her head, cherishing our time together. I didn't know if Destiny would come outside and snatch her away from me or if she would allow us time to catch up. She'd been unpredictable for the past month.

"Hey Jacob, man, I didn't know you would be here. Does Destiny know you're out here?" Worry lines creased Montie's forehead as he glanced toward the front door.

I followed his gaze to Destiny, who stood there glaring at the both of us. She looked gorgeous in a chocolate brown romper that showed my baby had grown in the three weeks since I last saw her.

"Come on in, Montana!" she yelled and Montana wiggled from my arms, just as her brother had done seconds before.

"Destiny, I want to talk—" before I could complete my statement, the door slammed shut. Just like that, I was shut out again.

Besides text messages she answered with short answers over the past three weeks, I hadn't heard her voice or seen her.

Missing time with her was why I fired anyone who even appeared to be involved with the sexual harassment scandal in my Utah office. I didn't have a problem paying the settlements. However, their insubordination cost me valuable time with my wife.

"Look, Jacob, man, I'm sorry for putting your business out there like that. I didn't mean to tell Destiny that you slept with Justine. It's just that when Destiny said you told her that I slept with Justine, I overreacted. I wasn't in a good place then."

"At this point, it doesn't matter who told what. The truth is out and now I have to deal with it," I said. "Nothing that happened in the past matters to me," I added, reassuring him that I held no contempt for him.

"I still feel like shit for being the one to break the news. It was your place to do that."

"I had brought her to Atlanta to tell her, hoping that us being where we met would lighten the blow. When she found out from you, I had to come clean. I never liked keeping it from her in the first place. I just didn't want to destroy us over something I didn't even do with a sound mind," I admitted.

"I know it may sound odd now because I ratted you out, but I don't have anything to do with it. I can listen to you and advise you, but at the end of the day, it's between you and Destiny," Montie said, his retracting body language matching his words. He looked back at a beautiful woman sitting in his car and stepped toward the car.

"Is that your girlfriend in your car?"

Montie gave me the side-eye as if he were sizing up my reason for asking about his woman. "Yes, her name is Lissa."

"Just asking because she looks a lot like Destiny."

"I know," he sighed, "It's just a coincidence that she's beautiful like Destiny."

"Yeah." *A huge coincidence.* Montie turned to leave, but I stopped him again. "I could use a drink. How about we have drinks at the bar down the street in about an hour?" I asked. "A drink amongst two men with a lot in common," I added, reaching my hand out to shake his.

"Bet. Let me take Lissa home and then I'll meet you there." Montie shook my hand, got in his car, and left.

****

Sitting inside Mundan's Bar and Grill, I told Montie the details of my 'encounter' with Justine when she tricked me into thinking I was making love to Destiny. We sat one seat down from each other at the bar enjoying wings and premium tap beer.

"I know how cunning that woman is first hand, so I believe you, man," Montie said and looked at me sincerely.

"Well, pray for me, Montie. Pray that I can get through to Destiny, so she will believe me too. I can't keep doing the hot and cold thing with her."

"I'll pray for you, man. No prob." Montie raised his beer mug to mine, giving it a loud clack. "You're going to need all the thoughts and prayers you can get with Destiny." He chuckled.

"Thanks, man," I said and shook my head as his truth sank in.

We sat and watched the game on the TV for a few minutes in silence.

"Can I tell you something, Jacob?" Montie asked.

"Yeah, shoot."

"Now that my heart isn't in the line of fire of your relationship with Destiny, I can admit that I understand the love you two have for each other. The same burning desire for Lissa lives in me, which has given me a second chance to get love right. I think you should continue to fight for her. Don't make the mistake I made of thinking things will work themselves out. The fact that I'm having a beer with you is proof that they won't," he confided, crooking his neck to the side to amplify his warning.

"I'm happy that you found someone for you, Montie. I'm already following your advice to the letter," I admitted, knowing that I had no intention of leaving my relationship with Destiny up to chance. I would spend every day of my life fighting to ensure she remained mine.

"Ex to ex, I hope I'll be able to congratulate you two on your anniversary soon, which means I hope you make it to your first marriage anniversary," Montie said and took a bite of his wing.

"I'll drink to that." I nodded and tossed the rest of my beer back.

Montie and I sat and talked for a while longer before we parted ways. For the first time since I'd known him, we had a genuine conversation where there was no animosity on either end.

Since I was on a roll with getting my feelings out there with the people who mattered to me, I called my father once I got back to the hotel. I confided in him about how Mom and

Martha's tampering with Justine and Rick's relationship led to her standing at the altar alone.

"They were doing underhanded things to get Rick's ex-wife to reenter the picture. Justine didn't even know the woman existed or her children, so it shocked her when his family and ex were revealed. When I found out Mom and Martha could be so vindictive, I had to talk to Mom. How could she think Justine being left at the altar alone wouldn't permanently damage her somehow?"

"Knowing your mother, Son, she probably didn't even consider the consequences for Justine. She only sees what she wants at the time," Dad said. "It's sad, but it's true."

"I'm sure they didn't expect her to kill him, but they had to know it would cut her deep," I said, and the tiniest bit of empathy for Justine snuck inside of me and simmered as I ruminated on our long, lost friendship. "While I was busy working hard at Turner, my friend needed me in ways I couldn't have imagined. She needed me to protect her from my own mother."

"Son, don't blame yourself for anything Tammy had her hand in. You had no way of knowing what was happening. I was her husband and I didn't know."

I ran my fingers through my hair. "I could hardly believe it when Rick's wife told me about it."

"I stopped being surprised by anything Tammy does a long time ago, Son," Dad said with disdain for Mom. "She can be downright low down and dirty."

"I've reached the point that I'm just disappointed. From this point on, I'm done with her," I said, feeling like a soulless bastard for disowning my mother. "I will not have anything else to do with Mom. I want her out of my life for good, and I have told her that."

"As your father, I can't tell you that's a good decision. After all, she's your mother and you know how I feel about family," Dad said. I could hear the strain in his voice as he reached for reasons to keep my bond with Mom.

"We're all we got," I repeated one of his favorite lines. "That's how you feel about family. Yet just because someone is your blood, it doesn't make them family."

"We *are* family," he said and paused for a beat. "Your mother and I were raised in a different time and by a different breed of people than I am and you are today. Your mother is not a horrible person at her core, but she has allowed the south's old ways to take root in her spirit. She used to be carefree and loved all people. Until the money got to her, along with the views of our less palatable friends and family. Add that to what her parents worked so hard to instill in her from the beginning, and you have a good woman turned rotten."

"I'm not willing to spend a lifetime without the woman I love to live up to her standard. She has shown me on too many occasions that she's not willing to accept my wife and, with that in mind, there's nothing left for me to say to her."

"She's still your mother, though. We're only blessed with one."

"My decision is final. I'm never speaking to her again."

"While I don't like what I'm hearing, I understand your outrage over what she has done to Destiny, and poor Justine looks up to her and doesn't know what hit her. Maybe you shouldn't focus on Tammy for a while, anyway. Continue to fight for what's important to you, and that's getting your wife back and keeping her. That's more than I did back in the Jim Crow days," his voice trailed off. I knew he was thinking of his relationship with Mrs. Clara.

"Dad, I didn't cheat on Destiny."

"I believed you the first time you told me what happened. You don't have to prove it to me. Prove it to Destiny. I'm already on your side and rooting for you to get the love you deserve," he encouraged me, and I could tell Mrs. Clara was around when he added in a softer tone, "Just like I did."

"Thanks, Dad."

"Talk to you soon, Son."

Mrs. Clara's voice buzzed in the background, saying, "Hello, Jacob. Go make things right with my daughter."

"Tell Mrs. Clara I said hello and will do just that. Talk to you guys soon." I smiled, hung up, and the brief elation from talking to Dad faded when it dawned on me that I would be spending another night without Destiny.

109

## Chapter Twelve

## Jacob

### I Belong to You

A week later, I parked in front of her house. Through the sheer curtains in the living room, I saw a silhouette showing the beautiful statue of my wife with her hand resting on the small bump that was our unborn child. She peaked out and closed the curtains quickly.

*She saw me.*

A few moments of anxiety rushed over me as I opened my car door and stood inside it, staring up at her two-story home.

The front door opened and Destiny walked out. The wind brushed her wet hair gently away from her shoulders as she strolled to the edge of the porch, her hand still resting protectively over our baby.

My slacks tightened around my groin at the sight of her radiance under the late-night moon. She wore a long, purple robe that covered way too much of her body.

A month ago, I came by and we both needed each other. I made love to her, and she threw me out afterwards.

Since then, she had shut me out. I came by every day since I arrived from Utah, but she gave me the cold shoulder.

I was fed up with missing her. I had enough. I missed too much of her pregnancy already. I refused to go another day without her.

I slammed the door to my car and stalked to her with a mission.

"You should really stop stalking me before I file for divorce and make it official," she threatened and folded her arms across her chest to put me at the disadvantage of not being able to hug her.

Standing in front of her on the porch, I said, "I wouldn't have to go to such extremes if you would just forgive me and let's move forward." I turned her face to look at me. "Divorce is out of the question, okay? I won't sign for it."

She turned away from me again. "Jacob, why are you here?"

"Why did you come outside?" The past few times I came over, she ignored me, didn't answer the door, or asked me to leave as soon as she saw me.

"I don't know," she said and ran her hands over her arms to warm them. "I guess I just wanted to let you know that I'm still pissed at you," she said, tears welling behind her eyes, ripping my heart out of my chest.

"I know, baby," I stepped toward her and she pushed me away.

"No, don't touch me. That's not going to help how I feel. You betrayed me!"

"Destiny," I ignored her protests and pulled her into an embrace.

"Jacob, you slept with her, knowing how badly she treated me. She put me in the hospital, disrespected me at every turn, and you slept with her in our house."

"I won't try to make my case about what actually happened. You heard my version, and you've chosen not to believe it. So, all I can do is try to get you to understand how much I love you and will never let anything like this happen to us again."

"Jacob, I want to believe you."

"Trust me then, baby, and let's be together and love each other like we vowed to do when we got married."

Destiny walked to the other end of the porch and stood by a swing. "Our love has driven me crazy from day one. I never understood why you could get me to do things no other man has been able to do."

"That's because we're meant to be." I trailed her and wrapped my arms around her waist from behind. I closed my eyes and basked in the feeling of our baby bump in the palms of my hands. "You hold the key to my heart. No one has ever done that but you."

She spun in my arms and faced me. "I only want to be with you, but I just feel so—"

"No buts. You are the love of my life, period." I dipped down and tugged her bottom lip into my mouth before kissing her passionately. Thankfully, she didn't pull away. "You belong to me and only me. I belong to you, and only you. From the day I met you, I've given all my love to you. That's what I will do until the day that I die."

"Oh, Jacob. I miss you so much," she said, grabbing the sides of my face and kissing me with so much heat that it felt like my cock would unzip my pants, release itself and ravish her without my assistance.

I led her to the door. In one swoop, I lifted her off her feet and carried her over the threshold, kissing her the entire way to her bedroom. I placed her on the edge of the bed and planted soft kisses on her swollen feet. I removed her robe and kissed her stomach. Seeing my baby inside her drove me wild.

"I want you so bad," I whispered as my nether region swelled in anticipation of partaking of my wife's beautiful sex. "I have to taste you," I licked a trail from her stomach to her pretty pussy, growling into her sweet lips as I flickered my tongue across her sugary bulb.

She moaned and writhed on the bed incessantly. Then, she reached for me and pulled me atop her. She loosened my belt buckle.

"Take me back, Destiny. I can't live like this." She squirmed beneath me, sparking every part of me to life. "I can't take being apart anymore," I said in a low hum.

My pants weren't even down my legs when I eagerly pried her thighs apart and mounted her. I thrust into her hot sleeve with soul-reaching strokes.

"Yes! Jacob, it feels so good," she murmured near my ear, followed by huffs and puffs that were so damn sexy I wanted to bottle the sound up for later.

"I have so much more love to give you, baby," I told the queen of my heart. "Take me back and save me, save us."

I said a silent prayer that Destiny opening her flower for me again meant she was ready to water our love with another chance.

I was in a ravishing mood, but I gently stroked her sweet pussy. Easing out to place lingering, intimate kisses on her southbound lips, I asked, "Am I hurting you or the baby?" I never wanted to do a thing to hurt her ever again.

"No," she pulled me back atop of her and guided me into her dripping wet core. Her tongue swiped my lips and she kissed me to heaven.

I stroked her sweet pussy gently. "I can't get enough of you, Destiny. Shit," I whispered, along with other pleas to let me have her forever. I didn't know how long I'd last inside her ecstasy. Shock waves shot through me each time she sheathed my thick cock into her tight heat. It had been a long month without her and she felt better than ever. Taking a mind of their own, my thrusts grew urgent. I pounded toward release, unrelenting. I breathed heavily into the crease of her neck. "I'm trying to be gentle."

"Don't be."

Two words never sounded so pleasing to my ears. I let go of my restraint and growled as I banged her at a breakneck pace. I couldn't stop if I wanted to. "You just feel too good, baby," I said, succumbing to the frenzy of emotions swarming through me.

Loud moans escaped her throat as she responded to my rhythm. I swam in the lovely feeling of being received by the woman of my heart. Every time I gazed at her beautiful face, I had to fight to stay afloat amidst the drowning sensations.

Her hands balled into fists and curled around the sheets. She screamed every time I went balls deep into her cove.

"Destiny, forgive me."

She thrust her pelvis into mine, letting me know I was, at least, forgiven for plundering her sweet hole into oblivion.

"I love you, Jacob," she murmured.

"I love you more, Destiny." It wasn't a full acceptance of my apology but precious words I hadn't heard her sing in that melodic tone in far too long.

My pace slowed to a steady pounding. She raised her ass off the bed, exposing her spot for me to grind into continuously. That was our breaking point.

The pressure in my cock was released with a gush of cum coating her delightfully slick walls. Simultaneously, her pussy muscles contracted and released me at a rapid pace.

"Jacob! I'm coming."

Animalistic growls reverberated in my chest. Mutters of pleasure slipped through her lips that looked like they were due a kiss. Time seemed to stop as I lay inside of my trembling angel, basking in the aftermath of the love we made.

Drained, I lay on top of her, lapping at her lips.

"You are my everything, Destiny."

"I want to get up."

I rolled over and freed her.

She wiggled off the bed.

I stood up and wrapped my arms around her waist. "What's wrong, baby?"

"I don't want to confuse the kids."

*Confuse the kids. Hell, I'm confused.*

"What do you mean?"

"I don't think you should spend the night."

"I won't play the hot and cold game you're playing. You can't keep pushing me away like this. We just made love."

She had a faraway look when she replied, "I'm sorry for that too, just go."

"Don't apologize for what we just shared. And I'm not leaving you," I wrapped my arm around her waist, pulled her back into the bed and snuggled up next to her.

She had mixed feelings. Yet, I was determined to prove to her that only one of those feelings was our truth.

"We belong together."

## Chapter Thirteen

## Destiny

"Matt Wilde is going to be the death of me," Tasha said when I answered the phone for her the next morning at 6:00 a.m.

I cleared my groggy throat. "He must be since you're up this early calling me. Isn't it too early for this? Can you call me after nine if it's not life or death?"

Tasha ignored my questions and continued talking. "Desti, I'm dying over here. So, you know I said I wasn't feeling Matt like that, right?"

"Yeah, I know what you said."

"Well, Matt was at a company party, and I was spending the night with Cody last night since he would be home late. After tossing and turning on the uncomfortable couch for hours, I got into his bed, hoping I could get some better sleep in his room. And I was right; I was asleep within minutes of laying my head on his pillow."

"Hold up. Why did you get in his bed, though? Doesn't he have guest rooms?"

"He does have a lot of guestrooms."

"Well, why did you get in his bed?"

"It's one of those king-size sleigh beds that looks like it's fit for a queen. Plus, it was comfortable. I just laid down in it for a second and didn't mean to fall asleep. The next thing I knew, I had sweet dreams that felt real."

"Dreaming about Matt," I assumed.

Tasha gasped. "Yes, honey. In my dream, he pulled me against his warm body. It felt good snuggling against him. I enjoyed every minute of it. He kissed me and it felt real too. Then, his tongue went in my mouth and I was moaning and shit," she said.

Realizing where she was going with her story, I gasped. "Oh, God, please don't tell me that he was in bed with you and you didn't know it."

"Yes! He had come home early and found me in his bed. When I opened my eyes and realized he was in bed with me, I pushed him away and started yelling at him about getting in his bed and kissing me. He had the nerve to say he was just following my lead."

I giggled. "You were in his bed, though. Gosh, what happened next?"

Tasha's voice got mushy when she said, "Well, I found out that we've been crushing on each other and trying to pretend we weren't."

"Well, since we're coming clean about our men, Jacob came over last night and is still here," I blurted out.

"Hm, so he came over and tuned you up again," Tasha implied. "I knew you sounded quite spicy this morning."

I laughed. "I do not sound spicy."

"Yes, you do, and there's nothing wrong with that. It's okay to forgive your man. It doesn't matter if you sleep with your husband. If he makes your voice glow like it's glowing this morning, you should give him a second chance. No matter what he has done, you took a vow before God to be by his side no matter what, and no one has a right to judge you if you decide to stay with him," Tasha said.

"I'm not worrying about anyone else's judgments. It's my own judgment that I'm concerned with," I admitted.

"So what? You won't be the first woman in the world to have a baby the same age as their husband's other baby. It happened before you married him, and I know it's a jacked-up situation. I'm not trying to sugarcoat it. I'm just saying that if you want to take him back, you deserve to be happy. If Jacob is the man for the job, then that's just what it is."

"Thanks for the pep talk, Tasha. I will figure this out. But for now, he's here. I'm not pushing him away. However, nothing is set in stone. I could decide today that I don't want to look at him again. I've been doing that a lot, and it could be his affair or my pregnancy hormones at play."

"Yeah, you get a little nutty when you're pregnant," Tasha laughed.

"You're funny. Ha, ha," I faked a laugh.

"I just want it to be documented that I told you what I think you should do."

"And I appreciate you, sis. We'll have to get together when I go to Miami for a shopping day with Mama next week. She swears she needs me to come to town so we can dress shop for a ball that John is taking her to."

"Honey, are you up for that?" Tasha laughed. "Shopping with Aunt Clara can make for a long day."

"You're right. I can't forget to wear my walking shoes." Mama tended to bring meaning to the phrase shop 'til you drop.'

"Just let me know when you guys get ready to go. I'd love to come and hang out with you two."

"Okay, I will call you then."

We said our goodbyes. Since I was up, I went into the kitchen to prepare breakfast. I took out a carton of eggs, fruits, sausage, and wheat toast to grill. I began scrambling the egg whites and thinking about my first argument with Jacob.

*"I saw you," I spat.*

*"What do you mean?"*

*"I. Saw. You," I said through clenched teeth.*

*"Okay, you saw me, but where? And, what about you seeing me is pissing you off," he asked the questions, but his paling complexion showed me that he knew what I was talking about.*

*"Last night.*

*"At the lounge?"*

*"Yes! Who was the girl that was sucking your face?"*

*Anxiety ran across his face. Hurt entered his eyes. "Her name is Justine," he said as if that was supposed to mean something to me.*

*"Go on!" I said.*

*"She's my girlfriend. I mean ex-girlfriend," he continued. "We're just friends, Destiny."*

*I struggled to process his revelation. Part of me reeled from the news. I half expected him to say she was some girl he met, and it meant nothing. Or maybe he got drunk and found himself kissing some random woman. But no. She was his woman.*

*"Girlfriend?" I growled out as my right hand itched to slap the taste out of his gorgeous mouth.*

*He nodded. "She's my ex, and we used to live together."*

*My jaw dropped open.*

*"She's not just a girlfriend. You lived with her, too. You have got to be kidding me," I hollered as I looked down at the flowers clutched in my hand. I threw them at him and jumped to my feet. "You are a cheater, and that's lower than the lowest piece of shit."*

I didn't want to keep reliving the past and getting enraged about Jacob's actions anymore. Those kinds of thoughts only kept me furious. I didn't want that anymore.

When his arms wrapped around me from behind, I turned off the stove and scraped the eggs and turkey sausage onto a plate. I put the pan back down on the stove and spun around to face him.

"You have it smelling good in here, baby," he said as he peeked over my shoulder.

"Scrambled eggs, sausage, and wheat toast."

He kissed my neck. "Good because I'm starving. Where are the kids?"

"They're with Montie. He's keeping them for the rest of the week."

"Why so long?"

I shrugged. "He misses them, and they wanted to stay with him, too."

"Oh," was his only reply.

I took his hand and held it. "I will try to work on us," I said and squeezed his hand tight. "But that's all I can offer right now... that I will try."

He wrapped me up in his embrace and squeezed me tight. "Thank you, Destiny. That's all I need from you. I will handle the rest."

That morning, I stayed in his arms until my insecurity about our love drifted away.

# Chapter Fourteen

## Destiny

### *Mama Knows Everything*

I flew to Miami to help my mother shop for a dress. After she happily dragged me into what felt like the fiftieth store, I began complaining.

"Mama, we started dress shopping at 10 a.m. It's after 2:00 and I'm tired."

"I have to go in one more store and then I'll know which one I want to choose," Mama said as we walked into Nordstrom's. She had tried on at minimum eighty dresses already that day.

"If you haven't found the right one by now, maybe you should just skip the party altogether," I told her. "Nothing in life should be this complicated."

"Baby girl, you should know by now that I spend a day just looking around and then I go home and decide when I'm looking for dresses. What's the fun in shopping if you just go in and pick up the first thing you see? It's supposed to be an experience, so stop being a sourpuss."

She laughed at my exasperated look that included sweat beads on my forehead. I had dressed nice in a ruffled shirt dress, pulled my hair back into a long ponytail, and put on sunglasses and comfortable flats. My hair had frizzed; I shouldn't have flat ironed it since I would sweat it out, walking from store to store on every clothing strip in Miami. And my clothes were sticking to me though it was late fall and only seventy degrees out.

"You have no sympathy for the pregnant," I whined.

"Oh chile, a little walking around isn't going to hurt my grandbaby. If anything, I'm helping you both. What you should be doing is looking for some maternity clothes, so you can keep looking good during your pregnancy," she countered.

I draped my hand over my belly lovingly. Perhaps she was right.

"Oh, I can't believe you're having my third grandchild. You were always much braver than me. I stopped after I had you. Too much pain."

"Mama, I only got pregnant because I wanted to share a child with Jacob. I wanted to be the one to give him his first child." A piercing strike shot through me with the realization that Justine was the one actually carrying his first child.

Anger entered her eyes as she looked at me. "I know you wanted to give him his first child, baby girl. That's why you should have let me get my hands around that scandalous little heathen's neck when I was about to wear her out the first time we met. Then, none of this would be happening," Mama breathed fire as she spoke. "I don't want to talk about her. I'll get another migraine. When John first told me that she was pregnant and claimed Jacob as the father, I had to lay down for the entire day. I was sick."

"Mama, I don't want you getting sick about what Justine does."

"I wasn't sick about what she did. I was sick because I didn't whoop her butt the first time I saw her." She rubbed her temples, looking stressed. "I just get so upset at the thought of someone messing with my only child. You're the best thing I created. I'm proud of you for being such a great daughter," she said and smiled.

"Thanks, Mama." I cheered up. "I'm not afraid of Justine. She's behind bars where she belongs."

"It's just the thought that a murderer attacked you and was obsessed with your husband, so much so that she snuck him while he was sleeping to get pregnant."

"You believe Jacob, Mama?"

"Of course, I do. I would take Jacob's word over Justine Parker, Satan herself, or any of the witches that taught her how to ride a broom. Those women are so evil that I pray over your name every night before I go to bed. I say, 'Lord, You could've let me fall and crumble into a million pieces a thousand times over. Yet, You held me tight; each time I was too weak to carry on, You carried me. You now have my daughter in your gentle embrace. Perform resuscitation to her spirit during earthly turmoil. Hold her together, like no man has the power to hold. Heal her wounds like only You can. Fix and mold us all and make us impermeable with each repair. In Jesus' name.' And baby, that prayer works. God has protected you and my grandchildren and even blessed us with another on the way. He has sculpted us into flawed yet perfect children of God."

I hugged her neck. She had always been a praying mother. A trait I hadn't embraced fully but would start. "That's a beautiful prayer, Mama."

"And I say the same for John and Jacob when I wake up because I want them covered too. If Jacob is anything like his father, he's been bamboozled by Justine, and it just ain't nothing more to it than that," Mama said matter-of-factly.

"Mama, let's find your dress. Your prayers have us covered with everything else," I smiled. "I don't want you stressing over Justine. She's already taken something special from my husband and me. Her shenanigans are not going to hurt you, too." I pulled her toward a rack of black dresses.

"Oh, she's not going to hurt me. Believe that."

I shook my head. "I think this is the one," I said, pulling out a dress with a one-shoulder strap that had blue and black carnation on it and the other side strapless. It was knee-length and pencil style.

"I think you're right. This one is more my style than anything I've seen today."

"Let's get it then," I squealed with joy that we had potentially found the dress and would hopefully be leaving the stores for the day.

Mama winked at me as she held the dress. "I'll get this one, just because you like it so much."

I couldn't believe she decided to get it, and we would be done shopping soon.

While Mama was at the counter paying for the dress, Tasha called. "Where are you? You were supposed to meet us hours ago," I lit into her as soon as I answered.

"I'm in South Dakota with Matt and Cody," she said with too much pep in her voice. "Matt had to leave town on impromptu business. Since he already promised me and Cody that he would take us on the slopes, this was the perfect opportunity to have a working vacation."

"Oh, well, since you're out with Matt, I'll give you a pass. Sounds like you are just blending into their family nicely."

"I guess you could say that," she giggled, flirting with the idea of she and Matt being a couple.

"You have a lot to explain when you get back, Ms. Ski Girl. Make sure you take some pictures of yourself on the ski slopes."

"I will, and sorry I couldn't make it to shop with y'all. Tell auntie I will come to hang out with her when I get back."

"Yeah, that's if Matt lets you off *work*. Since you're having working vacations and all, maybe you'll have more *working* sleepovers too."

"Shut up, Destiny! I'll be free. Just tell her I'm coming by and to have some food ready for me."

"Okay, I'll tell her. Have fun."

"Thanks."

I hung up as Mama was finishing up her transaction.

"That was Tasha, Mama. She said she couldn't meet us today because she had to work. She said she'll come by when she gets free."

"Oh, so she has a man, too, huh?"

I laughed.

*Mama knows everything.*

## Chapter Fifteen

## Destiny

### *We Are Family*

Mom and I walked through the hallways of Jacob's childhood home. Many of his pictures still hung on the wall where I saw them the first time I visited. I followed Mom into the dining area, preoccupied with the décor of the immaculate room that seemed to hold so much love, now that Jacob's mother wasn't sucking up the air.

"So glad you could make it," Jacob's father, John, said when I entered the dining room fully.

"I'm glad to be here. Jacob wanted to be here, but as you know, he has important meetings in Atlanta all day today," I responded.

"That's fine. You're the one I need to talk to," John said in a booming voice that resonated with seriousness.

"What is it, John?" Mama asked before I could respond.

He stared at my mother for a few moments before he spoke. "I have some news about Justine. I visited her at the prison today, and while I was there—"

"You what?" Mama's hands flew to her hips. Her words sliced John's sentence in half like a knife. "I know you're not coddling that girl too."

"No. It's nothing like that. Sit down, Clara. What I have to say, you need to be sitting for." John got up from his seat, helped Mama into her chair, and helped me.

"This had better be good, John," Mama gave John a look that said, 'because if it isn't, your ass is lawn mowed grass.'

John planted his elbows on the table and clasped his hands together. "It's two things. She does not have Montie or Jacob's baby. Actually, she's not having a baby at all. She has never been pregnant. I got that news from the doctor over in the prison medical department."

I gasped. My mouth flew open, but I couldn't find the words to speak.

"Praise God! That *is* good news, John," Mama beamed with elation in her eyes as she raised her hands to the sky and clasped them together in a praying motion.

"That's not all," John said, bringing our attention back to his second reveal. "She said she wanted you to have this letter, Destiny. She promised me the contents would explain word for word what happened between her and Jacob." John waved the letters he picked up from the center of the table. "She corroborated his version of what happened."

"So, I'm having Jacob's only child?" I asked. The shock from his first revelation was still laying the foundation in my mind when he revealed the second piece of news in the form of a letter. The pretense of Justine having Jacob's child had hung over me so long and potently that it would take more than a conversation to wash it away.

"You are having my first and only grandchild." John's smile reached his eyes. "Though I hope it won't be the last," he added.

*Dear Heavens above! Jacob and Justine would not have a child. But God!*

"How did you get her to tell you all this, John?" Mama asked with curiosity written all over her face.

"Well, for one, I knew that young lady since she was a child. She was an angel when she was growing up. She never was this vindictive, evil person she grew to become. She was Jacob's best friend; when you saw one, you saw two. Her family pushed her to her mental limits, though. I didn't realize it was that bad then." He stopped for a long pregnant pause. "But the jail doctors have her on medication that is helping her think clearly. She's distraught about Rick's murder and the deception she has perpetrated in your marriage. She also sent a letter to apologize to Jacob."

John slid the letters to me. There, in black and white, was the written proof my husband never meant to hurt me, just like he said.

"She has also realized that her relationship with her mother is toxic. She knows Martha and Tammy were manipulating her." John groaned his contempt over his wife and old friend's behavior.

"Poor girl," Mama said. "I thought I would have to whip some sense into her. Now, I feel sorry for her. She never had a chance at a normal life."

"She was very remorseful when I spoke to her. She had already written those letters and was waiting for the right time to deliver them. I didn't have the nerve to tell her that Martha and Tammy made Rick leave her at the altar. It would only break her down further than she already was. She knows they are bad for her wellbeing and that's enough for me."

"Oh, Jacob. I should have believed you," I said, thinking about the groveling he'd done to convince me he'd been wrongfully accused of an affair. "I have to get back to Atlanta!" I stood from the table and picked up the letters.

"My driver is already in the loop waiting for you. The jet is gassed up and ready to go," John said, expecting me to run off as soon as I got the news.

I turned to my mother and gave her a warm smile. "We'll have dinner some other time, Mama."

She nodded expectantly. "I know, baby girl. Go get your man." Mama's cheeks sprang to the corners of her eyes as she bubbled with joy.

John stood and went to stand behind her chair. He massaged her shoulders.

She reached her hand to touch his while gazing up at him lovingly.

I kissed her cheek and hugged his neck.

"Thank you," I said to my stepfather.

"All in a day's work," he joked. "Like your mother said, go get my son and make his lifetime."

I ran out of the house with my purse trailing behind me in the wind. I jumped in the waiting car and headed to the airport. As soon as we were out of Mama's neighborhood, I opened Justine's letter and read it.

*To Destiny,*

*It's not a secret that I never liked you. Since I found out Jacob was leaving me to be with you, you have been a pain in my side. I knew he was a best friend turned lover that probably wouldn't last, but I cared about him deeply. I didn't want to lose what he represented for me, which was a safety net from all the ridicule from my parents and everyone who witnessed me being duped by Rick.*

*Jacob was my hero when Rick left me. I think he was just more so there for me because he didn't want to see me hurt. I felt he was my soulmate, but he didn't feel the same way. Still, Jacob didn't deserve the way I treated him. Neither did Rick. No matter what anyone thinks, I loved Rick. I think about him daily, so my mind is not clouded by hatred. My new medications helped me see how wrong I was...about everything.*

*I think about how great Rick and I would have been together had he not left me at the altar and how I should have just left him alone that day he invited me for a ride in his car. I want to take back the pain I have caused everyone, but what is done is done. What I can do now is come clean about Jacob.*

*The night Jacob and I had sex in your home, I snuck into a side window that had been left open. I went into your bedroom and hid in your massive closet after you left. I dressed in your clothes. I put on your perfume. I wanted to be you because you had everything I coveted. While Jacob was in the kitchen, I slipped into his study and put a ketamine pill in his drink, which he drank as he worked on his laptop. He went to sleep. When he woke up, he was in a trance-like state. He could move around and talk to me, though. I knew he thought I was you, but I didn't care. He called your name and said sweet things about you as I took advantage of his drowsy state on a pitch-black night. He honestly thought I was you.*

*No child came from that night, so you and Jacob can live your lives without further interference from me. I'm sorry, but it's not enough for all the pain I caused. Therefore, I will just plead for you to love Jacob in a way*

*I wasn't equipped to do as his best friend or lover. If I die in this prison, that is my only wish. My only chance at redemption.*

*I'll be repenting until the day I die.*

*Justine*

I folded the paper and put it back in the envelope. All I could do was look out of the window at the passing cars in a daze as I tried to take in everything Justine had revealed to me.

## Chapter Sixteen

## Jacob

"Is Destiny still in Miami?" I asked my father when he answered his phone. "I've been trying to call her, but she's not answering."

"No, she should be back in Atlanta by now, Son. Is there a problem?"

"I'm just checking on her. Maybe she hasn't answered because she's still on the plane," I reasoned.

"Could be, Son. After you talk to her, give me a call to let me know she made it safely," he said.

"Sure thing, Dad. Have a good night."

"You too, Son."

I hung up the phone, figuring I might as well go to my penthouse suite and take a shower. I had been staying at Destiny's house for the past week. I didn't feel comfortable being there without her, though. It wasn't our domain. It was the house she built with Montie. Until she was back in our home in Miami or something we built in Atlanta, I wouldn't be satisfied.

Henry pulled into the loop at the Marriott Marquis and let me out. I greeted the bellhop and hopped on the elevator. I arrived in my room, kicked off my shoes, and began to take off my clothes. I went into the bathroom and showered for the next thirty minutes. It felt so good rinsing under the hot shower spray that beat my skin in various rhythms. When I exited the shower, I felt like a new man. I grabbed a towel and dried off before wrapping another around my waist. I had just begun brushing my teeth when the doorbell rang. I wasn't expecting anyone, so I slipped into my pajama pants.

"Who is it?" I called out as I ran down the hallway to the front door.

"Jacob."

I picked up my pace when I heard Destiny's voice.

"Hey, baby," I greeted her by pulling her into my arms.

"Hey."

"You look tired. Are you feeling okay? Have a seat," I escorted her to the couch in the living room and guided her down onto my lap. My baby's belly had been rounding off since she turned five months pregnant, and I was extra protective of her.

"I'm fine, Jacob. I'm just glad I found you here," she said.

"I'm glad you found me, too," I returned, placing feather-like kisses on her cheek.

"I have to talk to you, but I should stand." She waddled out of my lap to her feet. The beautiful grin on her face was killing me with suspense.

"Have you found out the sex of the baby?" I asked impatiently.

"No, that appointment isn't until next week, and you're going with me, babe," she said. "It's not about the baby."

Whatever she had to tell me had brought the old Destiny back. I liked what she had to say without knowing the details.

"It's Justine," she announced, causing my good mood to evaporate into thin air.

"If she has done something else to hurt you, Destiny, I'm taking care of her once and for all," I let out an ominous warning.

"She hasn't done anything to hurt me, Jacob." She stuck her hand inside her purse and brought out a letter. "Read this," she said with that innocent, loving smile that she'd spared me of for too long.

"What is this?"

"It's a letter from Justine. But you have to read it."

"What is this about?"

"Just read it, Jacob."

"Sit down next to me and I'll read it. Only because you insist on it, baby."

She nervously obliged as I tore open the letter with contempt running through me. Seriously, Justine would be handled if she was still causing hell for my family. I had no intention of living with her bullshit hanging over my head for the rest of my life. I was not her baby's father. She needed to get that through her thick skull.

I read her letter aloud as Destiny sat beside me.

*My Dear Friend Jacob,*

*I owe you a heartfelt apology for the problems I have caused you and your new family. I should have let you go when you wanted to walk away, but I just couldn't let go. I felt like I would not only be losing you as my boyfriend but as my friend, too. We have always been by each other's side, and when Destiny came along and took your attention away from us, that triggered something nasty in me that I didn't even know existed. For my actions following our breakup, I am eternally sorry.*

*I have written Destiny a letter explaining exactly what happened the night we had sex in your home. I slipped a drug in your drink that put you in a trance, so you are not crazy when you say you thought I was Destiny. I was wrong to take from you what you would have never given me. I felt so desperate that I wanted to have you in any way possible.*

139

*I now feel demoralized and sorrowful for everything I have done. I hope you can find it in your heart to forgive me. I know we will never be friends again, but your forgiveness would ease the heavy load on my heart.*

*I'm taking psychiatric medications now and have a huge sense of remorse for all the devastation I have caused in your, Destiny, Rick and his family's lives. I can't undo my wrongs, but I can come clean. I'm not pregnant, so you don't have to imagine a life where you would be attached to me for any reason. I wish you the best from this day forward.*

*Your friend eternally... even though I didn't know how to show it,*
*Justine*

"Wow!" Jacob repeated several times as the letter slipped from his hands onto the floor. "She drugged me. I never would have slept with her. There was no way anyone could convince me that I did it consciously."

"I should have believed you. I'm so sorry for not trusting you, Jacob."

"Trust is paramount from here on out, Destiny. Still, this is not your fault. The onus is on Justine. We all were deceived. No one in their right mind would believe my story. Hell, sometimes, I didn't know if I had all the details of that night straight."

"Technically, she raped you, Jacob, which could be another charge on her record, if you were to press it," Destiny suggested.

"No, she seems to have learned her lesson and is already serving time for Rick's murder. Besides, I don't want the attention. What I want is my family back. With the stress of her faking a pregnancy and trying to tear us apart over, I just want to get back to us. Can we do that?" I asked, looking into my wife's guilt-filled eyes.

She nodded. "We can do that."

"Good, and I want that guilty look out of your eyes too. You have done nothing wrong."

"I can't help but feel I owe you so much for not trusting you."

I raised a brow. "Well, now that you mention it, and since you feel you owe me something, I could use some makeup sex?"

"Jacob!" She pressed a finger into my arm "This is not the time to have sex."

"There is never not a good time to have sex with you." I laughed as I pulled her back into my lap and kissed her. "I love you with all my heart," I said and affixed my lips to hers, where I wanted to remain forever.

The passion grew thickly inside my pajama pants. My hand was already taking a seductive journey underneath her dress and inside her panties.

"I love you too, Jacob. With all my heart," she said and clasped her legs together when I slipped a finger into her wetness.

"Can I have you?" I asked because I wanted to hear her desires fall from her lips.

"Yes, please," she said, appearing in an otherworldly daze.

I stood with her in my arms and carried her into the bedroom. I couldn't wait to unite with my wife without inhibitions hanging over us like a putrid cloud.

## Epilogue
## Jacob

### *My Girl*

### Four Months Later...

Everything went so wrong that we had to start over to make it right. Therefore, I had Mrs. Jefferson help me arrange a simple surprise reunion wedding outside Tazi's. It wasn't a full year since we married, but we had a lot to rekindle.

My lovely twice bride beamed with joy when she saw the roses that lined the sidewalk and the makeshift canopy erected for our ceremony. The ebullience radiating from Destiny transmitted to every person standing on the street corner watching our unconventional moment.

Destiny looked radiant in an all-white sleeveless brocade gown with a veil made of satin lined with fresh flowers. Junior was dressed in a cream-colored tailored suit. Montana wore a matching cream color with a dress that matched her mother's.

Destiny smiled as she recited her impromptu vows to me, which included part of her *"Want Me Like You Used To"* poem she performed at the poetry club months ago. I assured her with Dylan Scott's song, *"My Girl,"* that I would do better

143

than want her like I used to; I would overwhelm her with love for the rest of her days.

The crowd erupted with laughter when I began to sing the song as part of my vows to her. People who knew the song sang along.

*She looks so pretty with no makeup on*
*You should hear her talking to her mama on the phone*

Mrs. Clara touched her heart and a tear slipped from her eye when I sang that line.

*I love it when she raps to an Eminem song*
*That's my girl*
*Man, her eyes really drive me crazy*
*You should see her smile when she rubs her belly with my baby*
*I can honestly say that she saved me*
*My girl*

Destiny's beaming face slowly slipped into a wild-eyed frown as I sang my country boy song. Then, she doubled over and lifted her dress to reveal a pool of water underneath her.

My eyes grew the size of half dollars when she yelled, "It's the baby!"

I held her up and uttered, "We aren't due for another two weeks."

"No, Jacob. It's time now," she yelled, and everyone started panicking.

"Pull the car around, Henry. We have to get to the hospital," I said to Henry, who stood beside me in a white tux that matched mine.

"It's going to be alright, Son. Just stay calm," Dad consoled me. I needed it because I was about to lose my shit. "You guys will make it to the hospital in time, and the baby will be fine," he added as I loaded Destiny into the back of a stretched Cadillac that was supposed to take us away to our second honeymoon.

"We're right behind you, Destiny." Mrs. Clara screamed.

"Step on it, Henry! My baby boy is about to make his debut into the world," I said, elated that I was about to be a father.

Destiny grabbed my hand into hers and squeezed tight. "Jacob Jr. is coming, Jacob," she smiled, "I'm having your first baby."

"I know, baby. And this is the best day of my life."


The End

Join Us! Shani's Imperial Reading Group is accepting new members. We have a blast talking about books, sharing quotes and hunks like Jacob, posting giveaways, free excerpts and prequels.

Don't miss out on the fun!

~Shani

**Want to read more from the Breathless crew?**

When  Tasha Baker loses her job, her friend hooks her up with a babysitting gig for entertainment lawyer Matt Wilde. Sparks fly between the bachelor and Tasha, but she only needs to pay her bills, good benefits, and to stay out of Matt's way.

Tasha is feisty, passionate, and everything Matthew Wilde needs. The more he's around her, the more wildly in love he falls. Before he knows it, he's ready to offer her the most meaningful job of her life...to be his wife.

When the word gets out in Miami's entertainment industry that Matt has a new woman, all hell breaks loose. Women come out strong to fight for Tasha's new position. Will Matt and Tasha be able to handle the firebrands coming to destroy their new love, or will the contents of a leaked video tear them apart?

**Part 6 is Available now on Amazon**

www.ingramcontent.com/pod-product-compliance
Lightning Source LLC
Chambersburg PA
CBHW071348170626
46811CB00003B/1034